Light Up the Valleys

Copyright © 2020 by Clement Masloff.

All rights reserved. No part of this book may be reproduced in any form or by any electronic or mechanical means, including information storage and retrieval systems, without permission in writing from the publisher and author, except by reviewers, who may quote brief passages in a review.

This publication contains the opinions and ideas of its author. It is intended to provide helpful and informative material on the subjects addressed in the publication. The author and publisher specifically disclaim all responsibility for any liability, loss, or risk, personal or otherwise, which is incurred as a consequence, directly or indirectly, of the use and application of any of the contents of this book.

ISBN: 978-1-952405-72-3   [Paperback Edition]
        978-1-952405-71-6   [eBook Edition]

Printed and bound in The United States of America.

Published by

The Mulberry Books, LLC.
8330 E Quincy Avenue,
Denver CO 80237
themulberrybooks.com

Light Up *the* *Valleys*

BY CLEM MASLOFF

Part 1

Chapter I

Yie Evroe was unusually anxious for a young man of eighteen.

A blamus was coming to see him from the claustrum on the peak of the mountains. This was an unusual event in a dorp such as Canara, down in the valley beneath the spiritual community high above it. The purpose of the visit was unclear both to Yie and the aunt and uncle who had been his guardians since he was six.

The conventicle brother would arrive late in the short period of less than an hour of daylight at this time of year on the lower ground zone of planet Tegumen. Of course, up on the mountain tops the members of the elevated order enjoyed twelve or more hours of full light from the sky. How could they have any sense of what life was like in the shadowed lowlands?

Two different spheres of existence. Yie had heard that repeated again and again. Two different levels of understanding and feeling. Everyone on Tegumen know that was so and had to live with the unequal situation as to light exposure and availability.

Yie was a tall, slender youth with straw hair and reddish brown eyes. He had experience tending the flocks of ovines of both his uncle and other dorpers of Canara. As a boy, he had attended the local literacy school. His teacher had been impressed with Yie's quick intelligence. His mechanical skill and dexterous hands were noticed and talked about. The instructor, a brother from the claustrum, reported on this outstanding pupil to superiors. It appeared that a blamus was descending into the valley in order to make provision for the future of the gifted orphan.

Before full night and the galactic aurora fell over the valleys of Tegumen, the blamus was to present his proposal to Yie and his guardians.

The yellow sky above the ring of towering mountains had turned a brownish yellow shade when the visitor arrived on foot. He knew which cottage to knock at and was immediately admitted.

The blamus, a round figure with a circular face, wore a woolen greatcoat, the traditional casaque of the male clerics in the communities living on the summits. Lively citrine eyes glanced around from under the square black barret on his head. It was flat except for its three peaks, reminding the dorpers that he lived high up on the mountain.

Yie's uncle summoned the nephew, then he and his wife withdrew to the kitchen. When the young man entered the parlor, he found the heavy blamus sitting in the pine chair of his uncle.

"Sit down, my son," said the stranger with a calming grin. "We have much to talk about concerning your future years. But first let me introduce myself. My name is Emies Plasq. I am chief dynamist of the Zeviv Claustrum."

Yie gazed at him in silent awe, taking in his every word as the cleric went on.

"Young man, reports have come to me of your scholarship and mechanical dexterity. In fact, the indications of your potential talent are spectacular. Therefore, I have decided to attempt something unprecedented. My plan is to bring you up to our claustrum and make you a sort of prentice. You shall learn the crafts in shielding against galactic rays and generating iotic energy from them. There is no need to tell you how innovative and unprecedented would be the acceptance of a dorper for such a post. You will be the first prentice ever taken from the valley below us. Nothing similar has ever been done before."

With a bold spirit, Yie asked a question beginning to consume him.

"What is the reason for making such a change, sir?" he said slowly.

All of a sudden, Emies beamed at the young man.

"It was my idea and I convinced our Hegumen to make the daring experiment. The truth is that not all potential abilities are possessed by the children born at the summit. I argued for the inclusion of a wider number of candidates for the technical occupations concerned with protection from the aurora and energy generation. You will be the first test of my concept.

"So, I am offering to take you back up with me, if we are agreed."

"Of course," responded Yie with a smile. "I accept what is offered with great joy."

The blamus glanced at the horologium on his wrist. "We must start at once, before darkness falls over the valley."

Yie excused himself so he could go into the kitchen to inform his aunt and uncle of his immediate departure with Emies. Only a minute or so was needed for him to go into his own room and fill a duffel with his few pieces of clothing.

In a heavy windbreaker, Yie kissed his relatives good-bye and followed his new mentor outside, where the heliac had set behind the peaks of the neighboring mountains. Darkness was falling through the sky over the dorp named Canara. The blamus led the way along the upward trail, toward the snow boundary far above. Yie had never before felt such a flood of excitement.

Trudging through the white drifts of snow, the pair could see the galactic aurora gradually become visible as nightfall advanced up Zeviv.

Flares of red, orange, yellow, and green danced high above them. Screen-like membranes of light appeared and disappeared, replaced by new ones, on and on without pause. Many legends found throughout the single continent of Tegumen linked the history and fate of the planet to this eternal show of changing radiation. Iotic rays from above their world, clear and visible, reminded its inhabitants of the enveloping cosmos. The sky of night glowed with great waves of energy particles.

The blamus and his new prentice followed the rising trail toward the towering peak where the lights within the claustrum glittered forth. Their climb was long and difficult, as were most paths leading up to the high elevations of the oddly configured planet. The distance from mountain top to lower valley was measured in terms of leagues. Steep angles characterized the shapes in the landscape everywhere on Tegumen. Incline or decline meant enormous labor in rising upward or descending downward. It was no wonder that few individuals ever made the arduous journey. Lowlanders rarely saw how those above them on the sunny summits lived.

They were like two different worlds.

Onward the pair climbed in exhaustion, until they reached the stone walls and the quercine gate into the settlement. Not a monastery, it included men, women, and the children of those who married. A watchman identified Emies and admitted him and his companion. Soon the two were warming themselves in the apartment of the head of energy dynamics for the mountain claustrum.

Emies placed a handful of coals in the room brasier and set them afire with a lucifer match. He invited Yie to take a stool and sit down beside the warm flames. "You can stay with me till a place is ready for you. Since you are literate, all my folios shall be available to you. My plan is that first you acquire general knowledge before entering the induction and storage units. That can wait a time."

The prentice was soon sound asleep on a woolen pallete in one corner of the chamber of the blamus who had chosen him for special education.

Chapter II

All the next morning, after the two shared breakfast and Emies left for the duties of his post, Yie read in a manual on energy dynamics. New, unfamiliar concepts flooded his imagination.

- The ultimate elements of the universe are its centers of energy, the corpuscula. As the final location of all forces, they possess neither parts, extension, nor shape of any sort. They are metaphysical points, spirit beings whose nature is to move through all time.
- The fundamental corpuscula pass naturally and are always passing into action, without any outside aid except the absence of opposition.
- Corpuscula do not act upon each other. The action of each excludes that of every other corpusculum.
- The activity of each corpusculum is the result of its own past states. Each corpusculum is the determiner of its own future and that of no other.
- Corpuscula have no windows or doors by which anything may go in or out.

- Every corpusculum is a microcosm, the universe on a small scale. The distinctive individuality of its representation of the universe varies according to the nature of its activity.
- The corpuscula exist without position or distance between them.
- All of nature is dynamic, not mechanical, because the corpuscula that form it have but one basic ingredient, their energy.
- The galactic aurora is the purest form of energy, because its corpuscula consist of nothing beyond absolute iotic radiation.
- Corpuscular energy is the groundwork of the material cosmos. It is the factor found everywhere, through all of time. There is nothing that can be compared to that element, the basis of all existents. The most common form taken by these corpuscula is light, which can penetrate to the farthest reaches and corners of space and time.
- understand the nature of light is the first step to comprehending the universe inhabited by the human species.

Yie, as if waking from a trance, heard a rapping at the door of the apartment. He shook himself, closed the folio he had been studying, and rose. Moving with speed, he reached the pinaceous door and opened it.

The gracile, delicate-looking girl standing there appeared to possess a willowy vulnerability. Glaucous blue eyes peered at Yie in astonishment.

"Oh! You must be the prentice brought up here from below. I am sorry to disturb you, but I must find Brother Emies at once. My father needs to see him immediately, as soon as humanly possible."

"Your father?" audaciously inquired the newcomer to the claustrum.

She made a sour face. "Excuse me, but I forgot that you are still a stranger to us. Hegemen Nomb Aacn, that is the person I refer to. He is the head of our community and I am his daughter. My name is Joa."

"I cannot help you," apologized Yie. "All that my blamus said to me when he left was that daily duty was calling him. Where he is and what he is doing is wholly unknown to me. That is all I can tell you, Miss."

Joa's tiny mouth twisted into an unconcealed scowl.

"I should have known that you have no knowledge of the layout of the claustrum. You arrived only last night, I believe."

"Yes," smiled Yie. "We ascended from my home dorp in the valley, Canara."

She averted her eyes from him. "I have never been anywhere below, so I do not know where that is. Only a few of us ever go down there. And, of course, no one is allowed to come up, except someone like you with serious business or work of some sort to complete for us here."

All of a sudden, curiosity seized the innermost mind of Yie.

"Tell me, have you ever in your life met a dorper from below?"

"Never," she curtly informed him, then reverted to the purpose of her presence there. "Brother Emeies must go to the hegumenia at once. My father has an urgent need to confer with him."

"It will be my pleasure…"

At that exact moment, the chief of dynamics appeared at the turn of the outer corridor. Both young persons heard his footsteps and turned in the direction of the sound. When Emeies was near enough to hear her, Joa told him that the Hegumen was waiting to talk with him.

The blamus turned to Yie. "Come along. He will be glad to meet and talk to you, my boy."

Emeies started to walk further down the corridor. Joa followed, with the prentice in the rear of the procession.

The hegumenia was a high flagstone structure at the center of the claustrum. The trio entered a large vestibule, then a working office with colorful woolen tapestries on all four walls. A bald, bearded man with baby blue eyes looked up from the pine desk at which he sat with a number of opened notebooks.

"Emeies, I've been waiting patiently to talk with you."

"Sorry, I was outside at the condensator. We had a minor problem there this morning, but now it is solved."

The Hegumen, noticing the third figure, gave him a cold, stiff stare.

"This is the lad you brought us from the valley?"

Emies nodded, motioning to Yie to step forward. The baby blue eyes brazenly examined him from head to toe.

Yie wished he were wearing newer, more colorful clothing.

Nomb Aacn spoke to the blamus as if the prentice was absent.

"I hope that your plans are not ruined through bringing up a young dorper. Remember the old folk saying: born a dorper, always a dorper. But I will be patient and see what you can produce out of a young belower. What is your name, young man?" he asked, turning to the prentice.

Yie told him that, his voice full and loud, almost near to song-singing.

Suddenly impressed, the Hegumen looked at him with close, observant attention.

"Is it your ambition, then, to become one of us in this claustrum? Is that the dream hidden in your innermost heart?"

The prentice answered back as if fully prepared for the question.

"I have not thought ahead to any distant point, sir. My aim, for now, is to learn all I can about the technical system that shields our world from the dangers out of space and allows the harnessing of cosmic radiation for human purposes. That is all that I have in my heart, nothing more."

In anger, the Hegumen turned away and spoke to the blamus.

"Keep me informed about the progress this boy makes," he ordered. "Now, I wish to discuss with you some plans I have for energy use in the months ahead." He then looked at his daughter. "Joa, show our new resident back to his tutor's apartment. Then, return to the hegumenia, for it will then be about time for noon repast." He then addressed Yie directly, staring at him. "That is all for now, young man. I wish you luck and success. You are now dismissed."

Yie followed Joa out of the office chamber, through the vestibule, out into the open air. Overhead, the heliac glowed with a radiance that the dorper had never seen or felt before. Direct rays of bright yellow were reflected off the pure alabaster snow surface on the ground. A sudden sense of whirling struck the brain of the new prentice, unused to such direct radiation from the sky.

All of a sudden, both Yie and his guide stopped in their tracks.

"What is it?" she asked him with concern. "Don't you feel well?"

He used his hand to shield his eyes from the brilliant yellow glare.

"I am unused to so much heliac light. Our day is so much shorter than it is up here. We receive less than one hour of direct light rays, depending on the season of the year. Our daylight lasts only minutes. It lasts much longer on this mountain summit, and the light appears much clearer and stronger. I marvel at the brightness."

"You have never experienced anything like our average day, then?"

"No," he admitted with a grin. "There is so much around me that is new. I hope you will help me learn how to live up here, Joa."

With a face of flint, she made no reply, but continued to lead him back to the apartment of his training master.

Chapter III

In the weeks that followed, Yie became familiar with the receptors, accumulators, capacitors, focalizers, and ampliators atop Zeviv Mountain. Their complexity astounded his limited experience as a belower.

"So far, it is only the beginning," Emies said to him one morning. "You still have the condensator, transducer, and retroverter to study. And there is nothing as important to our safety as the last apparatus is."

"The retroverter throws harmful rays back into space," noted Yie, "while permitting the iotic energy to go through and be processed for practical purposes right there on the mountain height."

"Correct," nodded his instructor. "It contains the pulse repeater that allows it to act as a sort of galactic mirror, throwing back the dangerous radiation while allowing the good iotas to flow through. The retroverter is obviously the key, the cornerstone of all our energy operations. It is the device that allows us to tame and utilize the galactic rays of light."

"When was it invented, sir?" asked the prentice with evident curiosity.

Emies gave him a broad grin. "That did not happen here on Tegumen. How could it have been? Our ancient ancestors had to possess retroverters from the very beginning in order to survive here. Every mountain community, every claustrum on this planet has them as its basic cosmic shield. No, they would have had to have been brought here by our original settlers who traveled from elsewhere. There was no inventing possible on Tegumen.

"It is too bad that our early history is so murky and obscure for us, but that's the way it was back then. All that we have to go by is folk legend, which may be no more than fantasy as far as we know.

"But one thing that is certain is this: our forefathers journeyed to Tegumen as colonists with detailed plans, programs, and blueprints. At the center of their initial activities was setting up a system of galactic protection based upon the utilization of retroverters as radiation shields.

"More than that, it is impossible for anyone to assert very much about that early period of settlement and colonization."

"I guess that is so," said Yie with a barely audible moan.

"But I believe it is possible using simple logic to reach some reasonable conclusions about what had to be true at that time. That is certainly possible."

"What do you mean?" inquired the prentice.

"Well, if the settlers came with plans and instruments, that indicates that their original world had to be similar to this one we inhabit."

"Yes, that sounds like a logical conclusion to make," agreed Yie.

"But beyond that, we possess nothing more than speculation to go by."

The dorper felt great disappointment, but dared not express it.

A severe, unending blizzard struck the summit of Zeviv Mountain. Snow and ice appeared everywhere. Most work activities beyond the technical responsibilities of retroverting and iotic energy generation and storage had to be suspended and postponed. The complex machinery and devices operated in automatic mode. Yie was forced by circumstance to stay in the apartment of his teacher. One afternoon, while Emies had gone out to inspect some transceivers covered with snow, a knock sounded at the door of the flat. Yie was momentarily astounded to find Joa standing there, a large salver in her hands.

"I brought some food from the hegumenia cookery," she announced. "Brother Emies and you are in all probability tired of feeding on hardtack cracker and barley cake."

She entered, Yie closing the door behind her. After putting the tray down on a small round table, the upland girl turned to him and spoke.

"How are your studies progressing?" she timidly asked.

He pursed his thin, pale lips. "I have been slowed down some by this snow storm. It is a totally new experience for me. We never have anything like this down below."

"I envy you," she admitted, "because you are learning so much about how the instruments and apparati operate. My own education has never progressed as far as that. My curiosity has never been truly satisfied."

Yie suddenly thought of something he was thirsting to know.

"You must have heard and read quite a lot about the history of this planet."

He had to wait a bit before she replied.

"Oh, I have studied the standard texts. But my special interest is in Tegumen legend, the folk story of how and why we migrated here in the first place."

"That sounds very interesting," he said to her, "because we have a variety of stories down in the valley dorps. I wonder whether they are similar to each other or differ."

The daughter of the Hegumen seemed to be suddenly in a mental trance. "That is completely new to me, for I never knew that there were historic legends down below among dorpers like you and your people.

"Tell me this, please: do the valley dorpers know the story of the Yellow Hats and the Red Hats?"

Yie looked confused. "I never heard anything of that sort from the story-tellers I knew. This is my first occasion. What is the story about?"

His curiosity was aroused and burning as he waited for her to speak.

Joa appeared to him transported out of herself, to another plane somewhere else.

"No one remembers the name of our original home. That is lost in the mists of long time and memory drift. Far back in the past everything is enveloped in clouds of oblivion. All that is now recalled is the warlike strife and conflict between the Red Hats and the Yellow Hats in another world.

"These groups were the opposite poles of a bitter battle over forgotten metaphysical concepts. It is not certain which group believed in what. They may have differed over the idea of the nature of the basic corpuscula of our universe. One party, sharing our present-day concept, believed in the independent autonomy of each and every corpusculum in existence. But the opposite group held that the foundation of existence consisted of membranes of integers that were interconnected. Imagine such a theory! They fought and argued over corpuscles and membranes to such a degree that actual combat resulted, with wounds and casualties. What were the rulers of our home planet to do in order to avert further bloodshed?

"The answer they reached was the exile of both sides to an uninhabited world. That, of course, was to Tegumen. Special space carriers were then employed to bring Red Hats to the mountain peaks and Yellow Hats to the valleys of the planet we now live on. Over centuries of time and many generations, none of the Yellow Hat descendants any longer wore the hats of their ancestors. Only the Red Hats of today continue with theirs. All of that early history was lost and forgotten. But folk like my family are descended from the Red, while your dorper ancestors can be traced to the Yellow who settled far below us. Each people went its own way and lived a different life.

"A different culture, a different method of survival arose for each of the groupings. They had little in common, nothing to share. The social distance between them grew greater and greater, and the cause of the initial division was forgotten. Each of the classes became as separated as possible from the other. Even our speech patterns and accents of language diverged from each other."

Yie asked her the question that was troubling him more and more.

"How did the defenses against cosmic hazards arise on Tegumen? It had to be here from the start in order that colonization could occur in safety. There can be no logical alternative to such a conclusion."

Joa appeared to shake herself out of her self-generated trance.

"That is something neither I nor anyone else can verify, for it is an unknown not mentioned in any folk legend that I came across in my study.

"Excuse me, but I must return to the hegumenia. I hope that you and your master like what I brought you. It is roast of wild cuon, one of the favorite dishes in the claustrum."

Wild dog, thought Yie to himself. Not at all the game hunted by dorpers down in the valley. But he knew he had to appear to like such highlander food. That was his duty as a resident here.

"Thank you, Joa. I am certain that Emies, like me, will be happy that you bring us that special delicacy. And our talk together was so enlightening and interesting. Can't we delve into early legend again? There are so many questions I would like to ask you."

"Yes, we must find time for that," she dreamily muttered.

Soon Joa was gone, and Yie had many things to think over by himself.

Chapter IV

In a few days the weather on the peak cleared up and a large caravan of weighty gyags entered the claustrum through the main gate. Drivers guided the strong domesticated, long-haired bovine carriers into a circle, then started to unload the heavy burdens from their backs.

Yie stood beside his master on an upper balcony of the corridor on their building, looking down at the show being put on before their eyes.

"The assessors are busy collecting taxes down in the valleys, regardless of what the weather outside may be," explained Emies. "It goes on forever, for we up here would be lost without the contributions that they gather for us below. We cannot grow the barley, oats, and rye that we eat up here in the snow. Our weather is too severe and raw for any agriculture. We are beholden to the labor in the valleys for most of the food we consume. In fact, for almost all the necessities of living." He turned his eyes on his pupil. "So, I have to give a sincere thank you to the dorpers who help keep us alive."

Both men, the older and the younger, smiled beneficently at each other.

"And we of the valleys receive galactic protection in exchange for all these assessments of what we produce," remarked Yie. Silently, he wondered at the unevenness of this exchange for the belowers. It was plain to him who was receiving the better side in such a trade. This had been the situation on Tegumen since the beginning, for untold generations, without exception or variation. Cosmic protection for food and material supplies, that was the historic formula and equation. It made survival possible.

The chief of dynamics, looking downward, spied someone there.

"Look, there is Joa walking across the hegumenia. She does so much for her father, the Hegumen. He would be a lost man were she not there to run his household for him. She frees his time for the major problems he has to deal with, just as her mother did before she died."

"The wife of the Hegumen passed away young?"

"Very young, soon after the birth of their only child. I often wonder…"

He stopped himself.

"Yes?" said Yie, growing excited.

"I was about to say that Joa has taken up many of the duties of her deceased mother. But perhaps I speak too freely of what concerns no one but those two, Nomb and Joa Aacn."

The prentice said nothing, pondering in silence what had just been revealed to him.

Joa acquired the habit of bringing special dishes from the hegumenia kitchen to the apartment of the two technicalists. Once she brought pieces of a roasted chevrotain. On other occasions she provided them with the serow, a goat antelope of the high altitudes, and then the rare goral and the rarer tahr. All this menu was new to the belower named Yie.

"You are spoiling us with such fine food, Joa," the chief of dynamics said to her one day. "Both Yie and I will soon become two gourmets. But we heartily enjoy what we eat, don't we, Yie?"

"Indeed, we do," blushingly answered the latter, turning to their patroness. "Tell me, Joa. Were the serow, goral, and tahr native to the planet, or were they conveyed here from elsewhere at the time of the colonization of Tegumen?"

She seemed to look away for a moment, but then turned back to him.

"I truly do not know, but I can try to find the answer in the record depository. It might be there somewhere, in the archival material. But I will not know for sure until I make a search of the sources."

Yie had difficulty concealing his emotion of excitement. "There is some kind of document depository here in the claustrum?"

An answer came by surprise from the mouth of Emies.

"Anything old that has survived the decay or time is preserved in a special room of the hegumenia. Few know of it because hardly anyone ever uses it."

"I can easily obtain the key-opener from my father," announced Joa. "He knows that I have a passion to study and investigate our past as the people of the mountains. I know that I can do it."

Yie leaped forward toward what he saw as being a shining opportunity for him to learn more. "I would give anything to be able to search existing records. There is so much that might be lying there that could answer many questions I have in the back of my mind."

"Questions?" said Emies, surprising his prentice. "What sort of questions?"

Yie turned his reddish brown eyes on his mentor.

"I would only read there in my spare time, after the completion of my technical studies for the day. It would be a kind of idle hobby, not interfering in any way with my work in energy dynamics." He turned back to the young woman, addressing her. "What do you say, Joa? Could you take me into this historic depository of the claustrum to look around? I would deeply appreciate it."

The two young persons regarded each other for a moment, until Joa made her decision on the matter.

"Yes," she nodded. "It is possible. I will get the key-opener and we can both make an investigation there together."

The supper of ursine guicade was nearing its end when the daughter, at the opposite end of the long table from the Hegumen, made her request in a loud, melodious voice.

"May I use the key-opener to the records depository, father? There are things that come up in reading old legends that remained unexplained for me."

He gave a stern, inquiring look with his clear eyes of baby blue. "What possible questions can find solutions in that trash?" asked the Hegumen.

"Well, there is the question of the earliest venery for game in the mountains of our planet. How similar was hunting in that early period to what we have today?"

Her father stared at her for a moment before opening his mouth to speak.

"Very well. I'll locate the key-opener and leave it on my work desk."

"I may need it several times, father," she added.

"Take the thing whenever you feel like it," he murmured lowly.

No more was said on the subject that particular evening.

The following noon, Yie happened to return alone to the apartment of the chief of energy dynamics before his mentor arrived. The latter was busy with the fine calibrations of metering gauges at the shielding station outside the walls of the claustrum.

He was there less than a minute when Joa appeared carrying a salver with the midday repast. She sat it down on the eating mensal, then turned to her new friend.

"I have it," she informed him. "My father handed the key-opener over to me last night. We can now search for what lies behind the traditional legends."

Joa reached into a pocket of her gyag-hair coat and removed the large metalline object. Smiling with joy, she showed it to him, then placed the key-opener back where she carried it.

"What do you think, Yie? When should we start?"

He let out a sudden laugh. "It is entirely up to you, since you are holding the means into the depository."

"Yes, that is the honest truth. So, let me think." She needed only seconds to decide. "Tonight will be very good. I was only going to read some folios in my room, but I can go into the document depository with a tallow lamp. There is, unfortunately, no iotic connection into that room."

"No iotic saque that we can read by?"

She grinned. "No one has ever before used the depository at night."

"It appears then that we will be the first to do so," he said with a jovial warmth and lift in his voice.

Even with only tallow light, he hoped to uncover some hidden truths in the records and documents of the claustrum's archive.

Chapter V

Yie did not reveal to his teacher where he was headed.

Am I attempting to conceal this activity? the prentice consciously asked himself many times as he trudged through the recent snowfall towards the central hegumenia.

I will have to relate this to Emies later, Yie instructed himself. Now is not the time. It will be more appropriate later on. Things will become more favorable in a little while. That will be the right time.

Especially should I find anything of importance there, he told himself.

Joa stood before him as soon as he opened the great entrance door.

"Follow me," she gently whispered to him.

Through a vestibule, into a side hallway, the two of them progressed. Up to a solid quercine door, where Joa stopped and inserted the key-opener. Yie had taken the tallow lamp and held it so that she could locate the hole.

The door opened with a squeaky creak and the two stepped in with caution.

On multi-leveled shelves and racks lay books, folios, and boxes of documents. A musty smell filled all corners of the tiny chamber. It was a terribly uncomfortable place. There was a derelict quality about the room, an aura of abandonment.

It was the prentice who spoke first, saying "Let's go in and see what we have here."

Joa stepped over the threshold, moving toward a far shelf of the depository.

"If I remember correctly, the oldest records are kept in the rear area," she whispered to him.

Yie closed the door, moved forward with the lamp and set it down on a small study table.

The two of them gazed at each other a brief moment.

"I will get some documents from the top shelf for you to peruse," she murmured to him. "And some for myself as well. We are on the hunt for any reference to wild animals found on Tegumen by the pioneers, aren't we?"

He nodded yes.

But he had other questions in mind, as well. Best not to discuss them at this early stage. Such sensitive matters would have to wait until later, he said to himself. That appeared the wisest course to him. Carefulness would avert mistakes or trouble, that was for sure.

It took several hours of reading before Yie stumbled upon an ancient folio that nailed his interest down. As he went through the lines, he asked himself whether this was historical truth or only a work of fiction. Was it fact or an imagined dream of some kind? That could not be decided by any evidence internal to the folio itself. The truth had to lay written within the deepest meaning of the content of this particular document.

"The Story of the People of the Land of Bodh."

The oldest of popular legends holds that the inhabitants of Bodh had a supernatural origin. A Holy Spirit descended and mated with a she-devil to give birth to the race of Bodhians, who had a double inheritance from their two parents. It was an ambiguous, dual legacy that they possessed. Their lives had a double character to them.

The first king and his six successors were known as the seven celestial rulers. The next series of six kings were the earthly rulers. They were followed by the eight terrestrials. Thus, the land of Bodh went through a complex threefold series of rulers, as predicted by the most ancient of prophecies. This was inevitable and preordained, according to the wisest wizards among the Bodhian people. All of it happened the way that it had to, as destiny preordained. There was no free choice involved in any of it.

Four kings called the Mighty Rulers followed next. The last of them was King Lhato, who lived to great old age. It was held that in his eightieth year, scrolls revealing the truths about the corpuscula that form the universe fell upon him from out of the sky. Under his son, Namri, medicine and mathematics flourished. The land of Bodh grew rich and prosperous. New sciences were discovered. Technical advances occurred with increasing frequency. There were no limits to the prosperity and the scientific achievements of the intelligent and gifted innovators and technicians that were present in incredible numbers. Inventions and breakthroughs came about in growing frequency in this creative, ever-changing society. Life had an intellectual momentum and impetus to it.

But then occurred the Era of the Great Schism. The originator of this severe philosophical division was a man called Amdo. Some came to call him "the man from the land of the onions", but no one knew why that was so. It was no more than a custom, a tradition. He was a profound mystery to all around him.

His disciples were known as the Yellow Hats because of their refusal to wear the traditional Red Hats of the old priesthood in Bodh. A strict code of morals was set up for the new movement. They were prohibited from drinking wine. The upper ranks were not permitted to marry, only the lower strata did so. Their lives were narrow and limited by responsibilities and duties.

New puritanical communities of Yellow Hats were founded, from which missionaries were sent out in all directions to preach and convert. Many were attracted to the new message and adhered to that current of spiritual thought. An unprecedented enthusiasm grew among the believers recruited into the new system. They were inspired to superhuman, incredible achievements by their zeal and enthusiasm. Their puritanism was as extreme as could be.

Thus, the priesthood of Bodh came to have two opposing parties within it. This was reflected in a division of the entire population into two conflicting camps. Bitter struggles, even violent battles, ensued. The two sides competed in the development of science and new instruments. There was long disputation over the invention of machines to utilize energies in nature. The Yellow Hats claimed that they had found a way to exploit heliac rays, but the Red Hats characterized this as bogus and fictional. Quarrels and disagreement burgeoned everywhere. There was little peace and no cooperation between the rival movements. Tension and conflict prevailed in all matters.

The schism between these two schools of thought led directly to the ruination of the prosperity and well-being of the population native to Bodh. Never has the greatness seen of old been restored or recreated. Reversals and calamities have occurred in ever greater waves. Conditions spiraled downward as if in an abyss. Chaos became the norm in the land of Bodh.

Yie looked up after he finished reading this interesting folio from the past. What did it mean? he asked himself. One particular item seized hold of his mind. What was the odd reference to the exploitation of heliac rays? If it had been a possession of the Yellow Hats, why was it now lost? How and why had it disappeared? Did it suffer a death by disuse, or had there been some sort of sinister suppression involved? pondered the prentice.

That was a fascinating riddle. Yie wondered whether there was more information buried in the depository of documents concerning any such extraordinary exploitation of energy rays from the nearest sun. His hope, of course, was that there was.

The voice of Joa interrupted his solitary meditations.

"We should be leaving in a little while, don't you agree?"

He looked up from the folio in surprise.

"Yes, you are right. We can continue tomorrow morning."

He rose from the table, as did Joa. The two of them moved to the door, the tallow lamp in the hands of the young woman.

Suddenly, Yie stopped and turned to his companion.

"I am beholden to you, Joa, for what you have allowed me to accomplish. This is a debt that can never be forgotten or ignored."

The pair stared at each other for several moments.

Yie unexpectedly leaned over and softly bussed her on the brow. She looked up at him, first in surprise, then in contented satisfaction.

They once again stared at each other's face without fear or unease.

"Be careful going back to the apartment, Yie," she whispered to him. "We will have to behave in a normal manner tomorrow. There must be no sign or indication of our special project here in the depository. All of this must remain secret and unknown."

"I understand," he smiled. "The same time tomorrow night, then?"

"Yes," she replied.

They crept out and the exhausted Yie slipped away from the hegumenia. There was much for him to consider and analyze when he was alone.

Chapter VI

There was no reference whatever to heliac rays and cosmic energy derived from them in any of the technical guides or manuals of Emies Plasq.

Yie was in a quandary over whether he should bring up the subject with his master on his own. Would his interest in heliac power from a sun arouse suspicions about what he was thinking about? Would it cause him avoidable trouble? There was no way to predict ahead of time. Any initiative by him would be a gamble.

In fact, it was Emies himself who opened the door to discussion of that particular variety of radiation and energy, still unexploited.

The two were walking back to their apartment from the dynamics station, where they had spent the morning in inspection and calibration. It was Emies who began to think aloud.

"I have often speculated about the weak ultra-galactic rays that bombard Tegumen all day and all night. Of course, they are mixed in with the galactic ones. And during daylight, with what we receive directly from the heliac above us in the sky.

"Those rays are not as clearly evident as the others. But I wonder at times whether we are producing iotas from them along with the galactic rays we concentrate on catching. Are they included, but not separated or distinguished from the other type of rays, like the iotic?"

Yie seized the opportunity offered him by this statement from his teacher.

"Are we also utilizing radiation from the heliac without recognizing what its source is? Is such self-deception possible, sir?"

No answer came immediately, because Emies was still pondering deeply. When he spoke, at last, his voice sounded distant and unnatural.

"There are certain important topics that were studied a long time ago and settled then in a final sense. Those matters are part of that established area. When our stations were first set up on the mountain peaks, the questions you mentioned were brought up. Ever since then, the conventional interpretations of light rays and energy prevail. No, there is no actual heliac radiation involved in any of our operations. This is true both at night and during the day, when the orb of the heliac shines down on us. There is nothing but light and heat descending, without iotic energy of any kind coming directly from the heliac.

"Does that answer your question, Yie?"

"I guess so," muttered the prentice. At least for the time being, he tentatively conceded to himself. But the young man from the valley knew he was not finished studying heliac light rays of the sun, a topic that intrigued him profoundly. He still did not know as much about them as he wished.

Joa had some news to relate to him that evening in the depository.

"I convinced my father that you should be invited to his Settler Day banquet. It is the greatest holiday that we celebrate in the claustrum and is held in commemoration of the pioneers who traveled to Tegumen so many eons ago. There is nothing else approaching it. The celebration is our greatest and happiest one.

"He was hesitant to have you there, since you are not one of us by birth. There has never been a belower attending before now. You shall be the first and only one, Yie. Isn't that quite an honor? I would certainly think so."

The prentice grimaced. "But I have no fine clothing to wear, only what I use for work and study, nothing more. How would it appear if I came looking like that? I fear that I would cause myself profound embarrassment that would never be forgotten. My being present might create a terrible scandal."

Joa grinned with good humor. "That cannot be an excuse for not being there with us. There are no dress requirements as such. It will be a come-as-you-are invitation to the prentice of Brother Emies. No one will expect any sparkling fineries on you. There can be no excuse for you not attending, none at all. You must be present and enjoy our most important holiday."

"I shall have to be there, then," carefully concluded Yie with a serious, sober face.

In the next two days, Yie steeled himself for attendance at the Hegumen's celebration of the Settler Day, a holiday totally unknown to the people of the valleys. It had never been heard of before by the young dorper.

His mood was a desolute one, for he had failed to find any further information concerning the heliac energy in any of the depository sources. His mind had sunken into deep despair. He was frustrated in what he had hoped to find out.

In his everyday costume of dark brown, he walked with Emies to the hegumenia. His tutor led him into the great reception hall that was an integral part of the palatial residence at the exact center of the Zeviv Claustrum.

Festive decorations had been placed and attached everywhere. Red ribbons, wreaths, and decorative laurels hung throughout the entertainment hall. At the head table sat the Hegumen, his daughter, and the highest officials of the claustrum community. Males and females, both married and unmarried, filled the large space available. A solid crowd packed the whole hall. There was movement and noise on all sides.

"First, we take us some food," said Emies to his prentice, steering him toward a long table loaded with rich delicacies of many kinds.

Yie had never seen or tasted most of what was offered there.

The two picked up white ceramic plates and filled them with chevrotain, serow, and slices of wild pig. Barley and oat pancakes formed high piles. Coastal fruit transported great distances was available: pomegranates, mangoes, quince, soapberries, mammee fruit, etc.

Never had Yie seen such abundance of eatables. His mentor had to identify most of the food for his benefit since he had never seen most of them before.

With overfilled plates, the pair moved to the head table, where two empty places were set off for them. Joa smiled with joy at their approach, pointing to the empty seats reserved for the pair.

Her father appeared oblivious of their presence, talking on one side with one of his subordinates. No greetings came from him for the two new arrivals.

Does the Hegumen intend to be insulting? wondered Yie. But it was the daughter, in a fine pink taffeta gown, who leaned over to ask the young man a question.

"What do you think of our Settler Day? Isn't it magnificent?"

He nodded. "Yes, I find it extremely impressive. Thank you for the invitation to attend and share the occasion with you. I have never witnessed nor participated in anything like this. All that I see overwhelms me."

The two were exchanging smiles when the voice of the Hegumen interceded between them, the pair about to talk to each other.

"What do you think, young fellow?" asked the chief of the claustrum. "I wager there is nothing like this far below in the valleys."

Yie jerked himself to attention. How was he to reply to this challenge?

"I find everything I am unfamiliar with most interesting, Your Grace," he said in a polite voice. "It touches me to observe your continuation of old traditions in this way. I am moved by what is happening in front of me."

"Yes, we cling to our past and do not abandon it. That is what fills our people of the height with pride: our steadfast loyalty to the concepts and ideals of our hallowed ancestors. We must never stray from what our history has given to us. Our legacy from our ancestors is a priceless treasure that must be maintained and preserved."

Yie made no reply to this, so the Hegumen went on.

"Our distant founders came to Tegumen as pioneers who had to tame a wild, uninhabited planet. Their goal was to preserve and never lose the intellectual values that they brought along with them. That heritage is what we are assembled here to commemorate, as well as keep alive for the future. Nothing of our inheritance must be lost. It must survive and live on."

The glaucous eyes of Joa, fixed onto his face, seemed to be demanding that Yie break his silence with some appropriate response.

"Each individual knows best the people and the customs among which he was raised and grew up. So it was with me, sir. I am familiar with the ways and the holidays of the valley where I was born. But up here in your claustrum I am in a new, different realm. Today, I am experiencing Settler Day for the first time in my life. It would be similar, sir, to your climbing down the mountain to observe how we belowers celebrate Declension Day.

"Are you familiar with that valley holiday, sir?"

Taken by surprise, Nomb Aacn frowned and scowled angrily.

"No, I do not concern myself with anything so strange and foreign to me. Not at all. I have no knowledge whatsoever of anything like that. All of that is a mystery to me."

With that, the Hegumen inclined his head away and began conversing with the subordinate sitting on the opposite side.

Both Emies and Yie attacked the food on their plates with eating utensils. Joa dared not speak with her new closest friend. No more exchanges occurred. As soon as he was finished, the prentice excused himself to those at the table and made a rapid exit from the hall.

He had not felt comfortable at all in surroundings so alien to his own experience. How could he ever fit into a society so strange to him?

Was he expected to make drastic changes in himself? How could he deny what he had learned down in his valley?

Yie realized that he was never going to be a part of the life of the claustrum and its inhabitants. Their lives were those of a privileged elite to which he would never belong.

Chapter VII

The following evening, Joa had a question for Yie in the document depository.

"What is your Declension Day? I have never heard mention of it."

The belower laughed. "I wouldn't expect you to have any knowledge of a holiday unique to the valleys. It marks the day, lost in the fog of legendary history, when the lower areas of Tegumen were first populated by colonists. The facts about it are scant, because it was so many centuries ago. Nothing much remains beyond marking the date each year. It is an occasion for satisfaction, signifying the end of the long journey from our primary world to this one that we now live on. There is a hint of regret for the lost life so far away in space and time. But mostly it consists of happy celebration of first arrival in the particular valley doing the memorial to the event.

"I would not expect anyone from the heights to recognize what the special occasion is. Only a belower would be able to name and define what it is."

She gave him a benign look. "Let's get down to exact research here and now," she told him, lowering her eyes to the old, faded document before her.

LIGHT UP THE VALLEYS

Emies was not meant to see the diagrammatic sketch drawn on a sheet of parchment by his student. But it was lying openly on the top of the small writing table next to the cot that Yie slept on.

The young man who drew it walked into the bedroom to find the chief of energy dynamics looking it over. The two stood and stared at each other for several uneasy moments.

"I am trying to make out what this might be," said the older man. "It appears to resemble some system of relay stations positioned on a vertical axis of some sort. That is what I make out on it."

Yie decided to reveal the truth about what he was creating in his mind.

"I tried to speculate about what a network of transponders to transport energy might be like some day. My objective was to predict what might be the system to bring iotic power to the valleys of Tegumen.

"Perhaps my imagination ran wildly away from me, I don't know. So it may be more fantasy than usable science or technology. Who can say?"

Emies put the sheet back where he had found it, then focused his citrine eyes on the youth with a mind full of dreams.

"There are problems impossible of solution for the realization of such a plan," slowly asserted the energy chief. "It would take energy to transport energy. There would be a vastly expensive use of iotas to achieve that. That can never be spared, because the energy is so precious and difficult to obtain. It is too bad that you cannot solve the economic burden of all iota generation. That would be very practical and useful and would cut the general expenses of making energy available. That is what our planet needs today."

Yie continued to argue his viewpoint. "But what if we had a system that went beyond galactic rays that are exploited at present? What if another source of energy was used? Is that a plausible idea?"

The prentice was on the verge of giving his mentor an answer, but suddenly held himself back.

What good would it do to cite the ancient words pointing to heliac rays as a source of iotas? How would that be of any value today?

Yie could not be certain that any such light was transportable down to the valleys of Tegumen. And advanced transformers able to change heliac rays into ordinary iotas did not exist yet. They might be constructed in the future, but were not available for immediate use anywhere.

The envisioned system remained nothing more than a pleasant dream.

Best to keep quiet and go no further, Yie decided.

As Emies left the room, the young prentice realized how little he had beyond a sketch and a few incomplete ideas. He would need much more than that.

A mountain spring emerged gurgling on the summit of the mountain named Zeviv. No new snows fell, and the accumulated drifts began a slow decline. Although the summit air was still cool, it lacked the painful frigidity of the previous months. It soon became easier for the residents of the claustrum to withstand the bitterness of the outdoors. But at night the depths of winter seemed to be making a return with their old sharpness.

The two young people, meeting each night to study the documents kept in the depository, came to have a growing regard for each other. Joa's feelings for her partner changed from unconscious to conscious, from secondary to central. What is happening to me? she asked herself with increasing frequency. She was experiencing an emotion novel to her, revolving around a single individual who was a handsome young male.

In the evening during the mountain's relative springtime, she discovered a report that startled her. She handed it over to Yie at once to read and study.

Joa gave him a general description of what it contained.

"This is a surprising description of how our ancestors moved about before migrating to Tegumen. Perhaps because we today stay in one location all our lives, it seems strange. But in the world previously inhabited by our forefathers, there was constant coming and going. An entire class of people were called the peregrines. These folk wandered and traveled everywhere, never putting down roots in any one spot. Always on the move, they never became a part of any single community or took part in ordinary common life. Isn't that odd, but interesting? I call it extremely important."

Yie, with a wide smile on his face, gave her a tender look of affection.

"What freedom those wanderers must have enjoyed! But how did they survive? What means did they have of making their living? What was their secret?"

"It is not clearly defined, but there is a suggestion that many of them were itinerant craftsmen of different sorts. There is mention in this report of unlicensed, illegal packers and peddlers. And there were cases of peregrinate tinsmiths who broke the laws with impunity. This is a most interesting subject that I never before knew existed. Did you, Yie?"

"Not at all. But it sounds like an interesting life, full of adventure. It was free of monotony and boredom."

"Indeed, it was," she agreed. "What could be more exciting than going from place to place, never certain what the morrow might bring. Always being surprised by the unexpected. Always facing the unforeseen. I believe that I would have greatly enjoyed such an existence. How about you, Yie? Would you wish to be a nomadic vagabond like that?"

"I can't say for sure. Do you know what the hazards involved might turn out to be? What dangers and uncertainties may hang over the open road for those peregrines? Those may be greater than anyone like you can imagine them to be, my friend. They might be the source of enormous difficulties. Who can say?"

She frowned at him."What do you think I would imagine? What do you think I am, a bird or something in the isolation of a cage? A trogon kept in captivity for its colorful plumage? I may not have traveled or seen much of our planet, but I am prepared to face any potential hazard out there. I can see myself in the years ahead as a possible peregrine. Yes, I know that I have the character and stamina for any hardships it entails. There is no doubt in my mind that I have the capability for it. How about you, Yie? Are you strong enough to join me out there in the open?"

Both of them were astonished at the words emerging out of her mouth as she spoke. Had Joa temporarily lost control of herself? What had taken hold of her?

Yie gave a loud, powerful guffaw that surprised her completely.

"Of course, I could do that, if you were with me out there on the road, Joa. Alone, it might be too hard to try. But the two of us together might stand a high chance of survival. Yes, we both might make successful nomads."

"You aren't just saying that to please?" she grinned at him.

"No. I mean what I just told you, Joa."

She gazed over at him, comprehending the implications of his words.

"Let's get back to what we were doing, Yie."

Both of them did exactly that.

Chapter VIII

Violent, strong turbulence arrived that spring to the aurora that enveloped the planet Tegumen. An unprecedented quantity of galactic radiation descended on all the mountain stations, including the one at Zeviv. More iotic energy than ever before was being created every day and night. A highly tense static seemed to permeate the air all about. The iotic meters and energy gauges registered that a flooding overflow was in progress. Nothing this severe had ever happened before.

"Some nearby star is going through a cyclonic convulsion, that is all," opined the chief of dynamics. Emies was sitting with his understudy at the circular table in their apartment. He appeared to be in a contemplative mood as they waited for Joa to arrive with their midday meals.

"If you are going to become my official assistant, as I hope, then you must become accustomed to these occasional eruptions and outbursts in outer space. They are part of the overall order of our universe. There is nothing any of us can do about them." He smiled calmly at Yie. "There is no possible explanation or rationalization. These happen, and that is that. We must live with them, because they are inevitable."

The prentice frowned. "Must we, then, always submit to what Nature decrees for us?"

"What are you thinking of, Yie? That insane scheme of yours for the diversion of iotic energy to the lower altitudes, perhaps?" He gave his pupil a quizzical look.

What shall I say now? pondered the belower to himself, his mind going far beyond what his instructor seemed to be implying with his question.

But before he could decide how to reply, Joa appeared in the doorway of the apartment, carrying their repast to them on a metalline tray.

Yie was thankful that he was saved from having to devise any detailed, lengthy explanation of where his thoughts were leading him. He was not too certain where that might be himself.

—

Rain, rare and unusual up at the heights, began to fall in torrents over the claustrum. Strange and unsettling was this precipitation, so different from the winter snow. An early spring was clearing off the mountain's terrain.

Few inhabitants could remember the last time anything like that had happened.

Some updraft of air from the lowlands must be the cause, many remarked. But rain would not interfere with work or normal operations. It must be taken in stride, said several wise, experienced individuals. There was nothing to become worried about. The snows were beginning to melt off the rocky surface of the summit. Never had it occurred this early. The mountains had always been the way they were for ages. No one expected them to change.

Yie came to the depository in the hegumenia building despite the drenching rainfall. He found Joa there, awaiting his arrival.

"I wasn't sure you were coming tonight," she told him wistfully. "There is so much bad weather outdoors that you were justified in staying away."

"It would have been a first time for me," he said, taking off his soaking saque coat and hanging it to dry on the back of the chair he usually used.

Joa stood a few feet away, facing him.

"You must not catch a cough in this damp chill," she warned him. "I want you to stay healthy so we can continue our important work together. That is important to me, and I know it is the same for you."

"I will begin doing something as soon as I dry out," he promised her.

"There is no need to hurry," she murmured. "The folios will wait for us."

She moved one step, then two steps, closer to him.

As Yie watched in wonder, she seemed to be signaling a message that indicated that the overture of their relationship was ended and that a new, more intimate stage was about to start soon.

Neither of them could say for sure what might happen next. That seemed contingent on a number of different factors.

"Your shirt blouse is wet," she said in a low voice. "Why don't you let me help take it off?"

He watched unmovingly as she went to his side and began to unfasten the laces that held his shirt blouse tightly to his left arm and shoulder.

At one unspecified moment, the unexpected happened.

The door to the depository flew open in a flash. A shape with formidable power and authority stood there. Both researchers turned their heads and eyes to catch sight of the Hegumen, Nomb Aacn.

He occupied the doorway like a mountain rock, firm and solid.

The minds of both Yie and Joa went blank in surprise and near panic.

What will he say to us? What will he do? The pair waited what seemed an interminable period.

Although something would surely soon occur, no one could foresee what it was going to be. Even the Hegumen was at a loss as to what he intended to do. The suspense reached an unforeseen peak of nervous tension.

His baby blue eyes, as hard as granites, focused on the half-removed shirt blouse hanging down from the body of the prentice.

Shock and outrage suddenly rose up the throat of the irate father.

Something was called for, Nomb Aacn decided. At last, he knew what the moment demanded. He saw what he had to do.

"Get out of here!" his hoarse voice roughly crackled. "I mean out of our claustrum. You are no longer welcome here, scum from the valley. Go back to where you belong, or else I shall choke you to death myself. Get out and never return. It was a mistake to allow such vermin as you into our midst. You do not belong in our community at all. You shall have to depart at once."

Yie looked at the fuming, raging father whose face had turned an almost purplish shade of red. He chose not to take the path of physical opposition or confrontation, but took his saque coat off the chair and began to put it on, his movements extremely rapid.

A glance at Joa made him realize that any fight with her father at that time would only cause her shame and distress. Her face was a colorless, pale mask without feeling in it. What was behind it, he could not yet tell.

The only way to protect Joa was to disappear quickly. That was the sole available means to lower the heat of her father's ire. Once he himself was gone, she would be at the mercy of the Hegumen. His hope was that paternal love would prevail over every other feeling in the parent. There was no alternative to leaving her here, Yie decided. The risk had to be taken.

The prentice made his way out of the hegumenia, into the pounding, pelting rain. But he was invulnerable to the brutally harsh weather. His attention was back there with Joa. Could she successfully handle her father's wrath? Was he sane enough to let her out of the depository unscathed in any physical way?

Yie climbed up the stairwell of the residence building to the corridor, then into the apartment. The snoring of the somnolent Emies sounded through the door of his bedroom. Good, he was not going to disturb or awaken his teacher. It was best not to awaken him at this time.

It took only moments to gather his clothing and place it in the saque he had come with from Canara. He was going home with nothing beyond what he had carried with him here. Poor he had arrived, poor he was departing.

Slipping out of his bedroom, Yie made it noiselessly into the corridor. The rain continued to stream downward, striking everything exposed to it.

He halted, because a moving figure rose from out of the stairwell.

What or who was it? he asked himself.

All of a sudden, the voice of Joa, softly pleading, reached his ears.

"Take me with you, Yie. I can no longer stay in the claustrum. We must escape from here together."

Chapter IX

The fleeing couple, soaked in rain, found shelter in an abandoned slope hutch once used by shepherds from the valley below. This was their first opportunity to discuss the future ahead of them. Both recognized the need to decide matters crying for immediate decision. They had to arrive at some shared understandings about their two futures.

"My aunt and uncle will take us in," whispered Yie. "But there is a limit to how long we can stay with them. Where do we go after that? I believe we should get as far away from Zaviv Mountain as possible. That is the only assurance of safety for both of us."

He peered into her glassy blue eyes as if seeking an answer there.

She looked him directly in the face. "I have been thinking about where it might be most secure for us, because I fear that my father will try to bring me back. He is going to chase us and try to make me return up there."

"Yes," muttered Yie. "We face his vengeful power if we remain too close to this mountain. I cannot predict what might occur hereabouts."

"Aren't there towns below where we can find shelter and refuge?"

"They are quite far from here. We have to consider carefully where we decide to go. We must not make the wrong choice of direction."

"You are right," she admitted. "Completely right. We have to make some wise decisions about what we have to do."

Sitting up in the hutch, the two of them napped the rest of the night. By morning, the rain had ceased. Yie awoke and slowly made his way outside, being careful not to disturb the sleep of his companion in any way.

The sky was a cloudless azure. The heliac shone from above, as it would continue to do for the next three hours. Short daytime was beginning to occur as they left the high mountain altitudes. The two were headed to the lowest levels of the planet, where daylight could only be measured in a number of minutes. Their destination was the zone of long, shadowy night. Light from the heliac could only strike there at a sharp angle close to the vertical axis.

All of a sudden, a small shape appeared in the meadow below the hutch. As it moved closer, Yie could make out the shape of a bent, ragged shepherd. In a few seconds, he recognized an old friend of his uncle, one who knew him.

"Binto!" he shouted with force. "Binto! Up here!"

With a beaming smile on his face, the herder approached. As soon as he was close enough to recognize the young man, he started to call out.

"Yie! It is you. I thought you went up to study in the claustrum of our mountain."

"I did, old friend, but now I am back in our valley once more. How is everyone? Has anything been happening? Have you seen my uncle and aunt of late? How are the two of them?"

The shepherd, in woolen work coat and knickers, came to a stop and stood before the returning belower, gazing with a wide grin into his face.

"I heard from others that your aunt had taken ill. An apothecary was called to Canara and your uncle purchased an expensive pile of medicines for her from the pill man."

"Do you know what it is she suffers from?" anxiously asked Yie.

"Mountain quinsy, I heard. Her throat and tonsils are monstrously swollen. It will be a miracle if the woman manages to pull through. The sickness is a serious one, very hard to treat. It is a malady that causes a lot of pain. There is little that can be done to treat or alleviate it."

"I must hurry down to see her, then," thoughtfully murmured Yie.

"Yes, that is the best thing you can do, my boy. Go down at once."

The two shook hands and took leave of each other.

Binto headed the way he had been going, toward a meadow farther up the side of Zeviv where he intended to take his herd of sheep in a short time.

Yie waited outside the hutch till Joa awakened and stepped out. He informed her at once of what he had learned from the mountain shepherd.

"I must at least stop and say good-bye to her," he concluded. "I owe that much to the family that raised me. My immediate presence is called for in the home that I grew up in. It is my moral duty to return and see them."

She nodded understandingly.

"Yes," was all she was able to say at the moment.

On the outskirts of the tiny dorp of Canara rested a covered-over wagon drawn by two equines. Some traveling peddler or craftsman, said Yie to himself as he walked past it with his companion at his side.

All at once, a dark-skinned man of unusual shortness appeared before them, as if out of the unpaved earth of the road. His posture was crooked and stooped. A peaked hat of several colors topped the head.

Large adamantean eyes sparkled like stones of diamond. He stood in the way of the young man and woman, blocking their way forward.

For some unexplainable reason, Yie refused to concede the right of way to the stranger, obviously not a dorper of the locality.

The little man did not retreat or go to the side as Yie approached.

A collision was averted only at the last moment, when Joa decided to speak in order to avoid what otherwise seemed inevitable.

"Look over here, on this side, Yie," she commanded him.

Her words compelled him to halt and look where she pointed.

"What is it?" asked Yie in perplexity, not comprehending what the intervention was all about.

In the meantime, the dark man in rags made a slight detour around the pair, away from the direction in which the two were gazing.

When the stubborn pedestrian was well past them, Joa decided to speak.

"Nothing of great importance, but I wanted to avoid any argument with the weird person who was about to collide with one of us. I saw no need to make a big affair out of who had the right to pass first."

All at once, Yie began to laugh.

"I think he was some wandering tinker, only in Canara for a day or so," said the dorper. "I do not know him and he does not know me. Those rascals like to provoke and challenge locals. But I was not looking to start a fight, Joa, believe me. Nothing bad was going to happen on my part, trust me."

"I do, but it seemed I had to do something to prevent a troubling crisis."

"Yes, I understand," he smiled at her.

The pair went on to the end of the primitive road, to where the cottage of his uncle and aunt stood, alone and dilapidated.

His uncle embraced and kissed Yie, but asked no immediate questions about why he had left the claustrum. Joa had decided not to go into the small building, but stayed outside at a distance where she could not be seen.

Yie stepped into the bedroom where his aunt lay on a high palette.

Her head was swollen, her brown eyes unseeing. She was unaware of her nephew's presence until he bent down and kissed her forehead.

The look she gave him was one that she might have given a stranger.

My aunt is so far gone that she fails to recognize me, thought Yie. Perhaps my uncle will tell her that I returned from the claustrum. It will be a good thing if the dying woman can recall who I am. The son of your husband's sister. The Yie who grew up in the village cottage, with you and his uncle.

The visitor held her hand a moment, then kissed her brow once again.

His uncle was waiting in the front parlor when he came out.

"Are you going back up to the summit?" the old man asked him.

Yie could only shake his head without saying a word. There was no way he could explain the trouble he had fallen into.

There was no need to give any elaborate explanation when none was possible. It appeared wisest not to say anything specific about his aunt's condition.

As he exited from the place, a clearer idea of where Joa and he were going formed in his brain. All of a sudden, his mind began to believe it had a conception of a way forward for the two of them.

Chapter X

Recent rain had waterlogged much of the gray canvas of the hoop wagon. The diminutive owner of the travel vehicle was busy wringing out whatever he could, using long sticks of conifer wood. He was perched on the upper edge of the side panels of the carrier, but not succeeding at his task with any success. This gave the young man who had nearly collided with him an opening to begin a conversation.

"Hallo there. That is a beautiful wagon you have, I have to admit. But too much water has fallen upon it of late. I see that you are making an effort to dry out the canvas covering. Perhaps I can help you with the task, because I think that I can reach the highest points of the top, my good man."

The dark-faced one looked down at the intrusive stranger. At first, he scowled in scorn, but then he envisioned making use of the stranger for his own personal purposes.

"Come over here and lift yourself up over the wheel, onto the wagon floor. Be careful not to upset the balance I've kept so far."

He reached down to take the hand of Yie and helped him raise his body on the narrow ledge of the wagon below the hooped canvas.

"Where is the woman who was walking with you?" unexpectedly inquired the shorter individual, looking about in all direction.

"She is waiting for me at the other end of the road."

The face of the itinerant outsider grimaced as if puzzled by that answer. "Don't you and she live in Canara?"

"We are here visiting relatives of mine, that is all," said Yie.

The wagoner handed him a conifer stick with which to work the canvas.

As the two of them moved gingerly about on the narrow rim, trying to dry out the fabric covering the wagon, the owner began to ramble on with a stream of words.

"I know not whether the dorpers have told you of me, but I am called Gev, the Tinker. My wagon takes me from valley to valley, under the tall mountains that soar up above us. What do I do? I make metal repairs and complete various tinkering tasks. I can work in either iron or copper. My skill are the result of years and years on the road, here and there, in all directions and quarters. Long journeying has provided me close familiarity with the layout of our land that very few others can match. I have visited almost everywhere, I believe.

"When there is a repair to be made, or anything to be renewed or rebuilt, call for Gev, the wandering jack-of-all-trades. There is no job too big or difficult. My reputation is an extremely high one, due to my time-tested capabilities. I have many years of experience that make me able to deal with any possible problem. There is nothing that I cannot handle. That is the truth, to which all my patrons can voluntarily swear.

"Wherever I go, my customers are satisfied. I dare to boast because everything I say is the truth. I am nonpareil, without match or equal…"

On he went, extolling the feats he was able to accomplish with his hands. Finishing his exertions on his end, Gev began to move his feet for the purpose of rounding the rear corner of the wagon so as to move onto the back rim and accomplish some drying out of the canvas there. But suddenly he made a misstep and his body started to sway as if about to fall over the edge, down to the muddy ground below.

Seeing the little man's lurch to the outside, Yie moved quickly and in the nick of time. He gently pushed back the moving body of Gev, enabling the latter to re-establish a supporting equilibrium again. The younger man stepped close enough to embrace the tinker gently with his right arm. The two of them looked into each other's face in astonishment.

"I am alright now and going to climb down onto the ground," announced the wanderer named Gev. "No need to hold me any longer. I have restored my balance and can move on my own now."

As soon as the arm of Yie was taken away, the other man bent his knees, then lowered himself over the back rim until he touched down onto the road.

Yie watched as Gev straightened himself up, then leaped down himself.

"I think we have done all that is possible," mumbled the owner of the covered vehicle. "You may now go about whatever you have to do."

This was the moment to seize the initiative, decided Yie.

"I must beg a gigantic favor of you, sir. It is something upon which the future of two individuals rests. Do you remember the young woman with me earlier, as we passed by you?

"This involves both her and me, and our common welfare. Would you be willing to transport us elsewhere?"

"Where?" asked Gev, a stupefied expression on his face.

"Nowhere specifically. I can tell you that she and I are eager to leave the area about Zeviv Mountain. Both of us want to travel to a town, any one. Where it turns out to be is unimportant to us. But my hope is that you will see fit to take the two of us away in this hooped wagon of yours. That is all we want from you.

"We shall be no burden whatsoever to you. In fact, I promise to help you with any physical task that may happen to turn up. As you have seen, I am quite handy with manual tasks. My labor, though untrained, can be of value to you, I do not doubt."

The now confused itinerant craftsman gave him a searching, skeptical look.

"How much money can you pay me?" Gev asked the petitioner.

"We are both poor and lack resources. There is little we can provide for our passage to another place."

Yie realized that the tinker was about to refuse him. He made one final appeal, hoping it might reverse the refusal that seemed immanent.

"I have studied iotic dynamics up in the claustrum of Zeviv Mountain. There is little I do not know about energy generation. All radiation from space falls under my technical knowledge and capability. I am an expert in that area."

For some unknown reason, this statement led to an instant reversal in the tone and mood on the face of Gev the Tinker. A distant light gleamed forth from the adamantean eyes of the decision-maker who possessed a wagon.

"Can you help me with metallic repairs?" asked the itinerant. "I have work promised me in tin, iron, copper, and several other substances. Are you willing to aid me as my assistant?"

"Yes, I am," asserted Yie, sensing a reversal of fortune in his direction.

He sensed that he would do almost anything to get Joa away from this region.

"I shall take both of you along with me, then," decided Gev, his mouth and jaw sagging a bit. Did he foresee possible future regrets?

"You can bring the woman to the wagon. We start out on the road at once."

Yie hurried away to report the good news to his fellow fugitive.

An unforeseeable adventure was commencing for them. Their future rested in the hands of a peregrinating tinker of the open road.

Part 2

Chapter I

The Hegumen of Zeviv Claustrum rebounded from a nadir of melancholy. He was suddenly filled with a vibrant restlessness to take action outside the walls of the mountain community.

His most trusted subordinates were summoned to his private office in the hegumenia to hear his plans for bringing back his missing daughter.

Sitting behind an iron desk, Nomb Aacn harangued the listening group.

"This concerns more than my personal family claims. What the prentice did was an insult to all of us. Stealing away an innocent, naïve girl is more than criminal, it is sacrilegious. Can one think of a greater sin than the one this belower has committed? A father cannot be a passive witness to such grievous injury. It is absurd to expect no vengeance for what he did.

"So, what are we to do about her abduction? I have already dispatched a small posse to the dorp of the criminal to search for them. If the two are not found, our people are under orders to inspect the entire area. No possible hiding place is to be neglected. Every spot must be opened up and investigated. They must be located and taken into custody. That has become the primary task for this entire claustrum.

"Now, I need more volunteers to go down and fan out from the dorp called Canara. On and on they need to go, looking in at every house or hut, however large or small, rich or poor. I can foresee how some will tire. So, we must go on to organize a third search team. There can be no stopping until they are found and Joa is back here where she belongs. Any weapon available, any amount of force, can justly be used to uncover this serpent and his victim. Expense cannot be a consideration. Nothing is as important or urgent as this search.

"It may turn out that fast transportation will be needed for the pursuit of the miscreant and his innocent prey. I authorize you to confiscate any equines that you need for quick movement in hunting them down. The search for them must be relentless and exhaustive. Not a rock can be left unturned. Look everywhere, question everyone. There must surely be witnesses to the path that the prentice is taking. Find and interrogate them.

"There is one person I hold culpable for allowing the crime to happen under his nose. Emies Plasq now lies locked up in the carcel for his negligent abetting of the kidnapping of my daughter. I have divided up his former post of energy dynamics head among the skilled technicals of the staff he previously managed. He no longer holds that office or fulfills its functions. He is one who betrayed all that our ancestors passed on to us. His crimes are unforgiveable.

"So, I will be awaiting reports on the progress of the campaign to return Joa to her home, where she belongs. That is all, for now."

The summoned brothers flowed out of the room in general silence.

Gev the Tinker followed the route he had used for many years, going from dorp to dorp plying his trade. Buying broken tools and utensils that could not be repaired on the spot, he gave his word to bring them back in usable condition on his next trip. His operations were a puzzle to both Yie and Joa, but they hesitated to ask him about aspects of his work and business that he might prefer to keep close to his chest. His secrets belonged to him alone.

Villagers provided the travelers with food, either bought by Gev or in exchange for the services that he performed for them.

High above, in the mountains, the snow melted away and springtime vegetation started to grow in lively green and other colors.

Each evening after a roadside supper, the craftsman did most of the talking, expatiating about the way of life of peregrinators like himself.

"No one can say for certain how we began or where we came from before the migration to Tegumen. All that was eons ago and is hidden in the fog of time. Some say we are the divagators or even the extravagators of our planet, because the entire world has become our home, or at least its land surface. We know all the valleys because we travel them. We have seen all the lakes and rivers. There is no place, except the mountain summits, where we do not go. So, our knowledge of the contours of the land is the fullest, the completest that exists. Nothing lives outside our sight. We see and remember every part of it. We enjoy complete knowledge of the surface land.

"When an outsider wishes to abuse or insult us, he often uses an ancient term, the Gitani, to label and define us. For many centuries, our people worked as Aurari, panning for and washing out gold grains and powder in the mountain streams of Tegumen. The name Lingari was applied to the itinerant woodcarvers and spoonmakers. There are only a few of them left today, for the craft has with time slowly died out.

"I myself learned this art from my father and grandfather, who are both now dead. We belong to a trade which calls itself the Caldari, mainly because we do our intricate work in a giant kettle called a caldarium."

At that point, Yie felt that he had to ask an important question of the little man sitting on the ground. A low fire burning between them provided a degree of light.

"You do not carry any such kettle with you on this wagon. What might your melting vessel be, then?" asked the fugitive young man.

"The one that I use is not mine alone. It belongs to our corporate guild of Caldari. Any one of us members is able to do his work at our great, central cauldron. We all have the responsibility of maintaining and preserving it so that the great container will always remain available to us."

"So, we are returning to that cauldron on the circuit you are at present making about this region?" questioned Yie, his mind jumping ahead.

"That is correct," answered the tinker, reaching forward with a large stone in his right hand with which to extinguish the fire. "It is about time for rest and sleep," he informed his two passengers in a drowsy voice. "We shall need all our strength tomorrow, all of us."

Yie's uncle opened the front door of his cottage to discover a dozen highland Brothers standing there in black mantelets and red birretas. His eyes widened and his mouth gaped open. What did they want? What were they after? Why had they come to his poor cottage? he trembled.

A fat, rotund man in front of the others from above stated what their mission there was.

"We must locate your nephew, the one who went up to the claustrum to learn a technical profession. Where is he? You must tell us whatever you know. It is important that we find him as soon as possible."

The startled old man spoke from a dry, hoarse throat.

"He is not here. I know not where he went after making a visit to our cottage to see his dying aunt. No, he said not a word about where he might be headed. I assumed that he was going to return to your place up above, sirs."

"Did he have anyone with him?" continued the Brother. "A young woman, for example?"

"I saw no one else with him, either male or female. He appeared to be completely alone."

In a second, the highlander exploded with ire. "You baseborn vermin! You dare lie to your betters." He suddenly raised his right hand, in which there was a small quirt, and started lashing and whipping the old man's head, face, shoulders, neck, and breast.

His anger and fury rose to the level of mad frenzy as he continued his assault.

Only when the uncle of Yie fell to the ground, unconscious and bleeding, did the attacker cease his savage physical attack on the helpless old man.

He gave a hand signal to his comrades. The group departed, their mission of finding the fugitives frustrated by the stricken relative of the former prentice. They would have to search elsewhere for the two young fugitives.

Chapter II

With only thirty minutes of daily light from the heliac, the hoop wagon did most of its road travel within narrow limits of time. Most light rays came downward in a narrow radius around the vertical axis. Each day was growing by a minute beyond the length of the one preceding it. The signs of approaching spring grew visible in the valleys the tinker and his passengers passed through. New light and warmth were arriving, welcome and satisfying.

Above the valley lowlands, the mountain heights were blooming with spring growth of grass, bushes, and flowers.

One evening Gev had important news for the other two.

"Tomorrow we arrive in the hamlet of Meridia, just in time for the vernal feria held there every spring on that date. I will have the chance to provide services for many inhabitants and visitors, and the two of you can enjoy the games and entertainment that go on. It will be a happy occasion, I predict."

The wagon rolled into Meridia in the hour before the heliac appeared above the adjacent mountain. Gev parked his vehicle near the grassy commons where the festival was set to occur that day. Fevered preparations were in progress on all sides, the three could see at once.

This was to be a holiday celebration for those who assembled here from the nearby villages.

As soon as breakfast was finished, Yie and Joa began to stroll about the fair grounds, looking at the activities that would before long have to end because of the limited length of the spring day. The foreseeable lack of time appeared to make the Meridians and their guests excitedly active, eager to have their fun before the rays of the heliac disappeared, before dusk fell on the valley and put an end to the activities that needed full daylight.

Young athletes ran in foot races. Swings hanging from tall pine trees provided thrills. A tug-of-war with homemade ropes occurred. Large leather balls were kicked and thrown about. Children indulged in repeated sessions of hide-and-seek. Old men knelled down to play at hazards with wooden dice. A group of locals had set up smoothened lanes for games of tenpins. Women behind long tables sold pastries and sweets made at home. A keg of sour alegar was being tapped, with the ale being poured into large primitive cylixes.

The pair of fugitives moved to the far end of the commons, where whole families of belowers were scattered on wool blankets they had brought with them from their homes. They ate flans and panadas, dipping them in pots of samp, caper sauce, ragout, salmagundi, and allapodrida. Winter pears and biffins appeared to be their favorite desserts. The signs of holiday enjoyments were present everywhere one looked. Faces appeared full of joy.

Spicy odors wafted past Yie and Joa, tempting both of them. Their mouths watered.

Feeling about in his right pocket, the young man took hold of coins that Gev had paid him for helping him in his labors as a tinker.

"Let me buy you some food, Joa," he proposed. "If you are as hungry as I am, some edibles would be most welcome at the moment."

But at that second something happened that prevented either one of them partaking of the food at the spring feria.

At least four figures in black, with red birettes on their heads, suddenly appeared at the other end of the commons, where games were still in progress. They looked about in all directions, hunting for something.

These were pursuers from the Zeviv Claustrum, no doubt about that.

Yie realized that fact first, Joa only a moment or so later.

What do we do? was the question striking both their minds at once. The two exchanged looks of worry and alarm.

A possible way of escape occurred to Yie as he heard the music of a gittern playing in a wooded area adjacent to the grassy commons. He pointed in the direction from where the sound came, opposite the end where the Brothers from the heights were searching for the pair they were after.

The two fugitives took lively steps toward the site of the music, passing through a small grove of quercines to get to a grassless open field prepared for dancing. A lively gavoto was in progress, couples circling about in orderly formations to antique tunes whose origins were lost in the forest of times past.

"Let's join the others," whispered Yie to his proposed dancing partner. "We can stay here until the feria ends. It will not be too long. Then, we can go back to the wagon of Gev."

He pointed to the falling heliac in the pale sky above. It was soon going to disappear. Darkness would descend over them and all the others. Night was approaching with its usual speed.

Joa answered him with a nod and the two of them prepared to enter the next round of dance, a simple quadrille with a slow, modest rhythm. These were steps that both of them could perform with sufficient skill.

The music stopped and the dancers dispersed homewards. A rapidly falling dusk announced the end of festivities to all the belowers enjoying themselves.

Their festival was limited by the half hour of direct sunlight from immediately above and the darkening twilight that followed.

Above the fairground, jagged peaks towered about in all directions. The highlands still had heliac light that was to last a considerable amount of time.

Yie continued to hold the hand of his partner. He whispered, his mouth close to her ear.

"We cannot stay here, but have to take a gamble that the Red Hats have left."

The pair made for the spot where Gev's hoop wagon was parked.

In a few minutes, they had safely crossed the commons to where their transporter waited impatiently for them. His anger had subsided, turning into burning curiosity over their tardiness in returning.

"Where have you two been? It is too late for us to leave now. Our entire schedule has been disrupted."

Yie decided that their story had to be told at this juncture. It took him surprisingly little time to narrate the main features of their adventures at the claustrum and their subsequent flight through the valleys.

The adamantean eyes of their protector grew large, then reverted back to normal. He spoke to them in a warm, sympathetic voice.

"I thought there was something like that involved, but I never suspected the seriousness of the matter," said Gev with evident emotion. "Do not be afraid. I know how to conceal and shield you, and that is what I here and now promise to accomplish. No one shall touch or bother either one of you. I promise to defend you from all enemies. I know how to accomplish that. You shall both be safe with me, I promise."

He raised his right arm as if taking a vow.

"When will we leave this place?" asked Joa with a shudder. "It is not safe to remain too long. Everyone is headed homeward."

"I can travel the road at night, in the dark. I will and I must. Our speed will be a slow one, but we will be going away from the adjacent hamlet, in a different direction from the one we had been taking before."

"A different route?" questioned Yie. "It is not our desire in any way to spoil your regular circuit, Gev. We must not interfere with your plans, not at all."

The tinker smiled at him with self-confidence.

"I can certainly return to my old itinerary later on. The place we are going to is called Rocumbol Mountain, the ancient center for all Calderi. That is where our iron, copper, and tin is produced in smelter caves."

"Caves?" said Yie excitedly.

"What better location is there to hide you in?" grinned the wandering craftsman.

Chapter III

Gev pointed out and named the various species of trees as they made their way into a long valley of thick forest. Quercine, fraxine, salix, ulmus, acer, and betula among other types were individually pointed out by the tinker who drove the hoop wagon. His two passengers felt increasing security as the distance from Zeviv Mountain and the claustrum grew greater and greater. It was becoming harder for their Red Hat pursuers to trail them as their route turned, swirled about, and wandered. Distance was becoming their protector.

Gev drew their attention to the large yellow leaves of the grindelia plant, the bluish sweet chervil, and the black hellebore. He indicated the trumpet-shaped spring flowers of the ipomoea, the common morning-glory. The natural beauty of the valley forests was inspiring and encouraging to his companions, in spite of the limited minutes of daily heliac light from the sky.

The passengers were surprised and amazed at the tinner's knowledge of local and regional flora wherever the road took them.

"I have passed everywhere many times, year after year," he explained to them. "My home is in all the valleys of Tegumen, all of them."

But then they reached a fork and an opening between two tall mountains that blotted out most of the darkening sky from which the light was rapidly vanishing.

The driver stopped the equines so that he could allow his comrades a clear view of their destination, Calderia Mountain.

"How green it is!" marveled Joa. "I think even the snow peak is beautiful. Can we see its claustrum from where we are?"

"There is no upper community on Calderia. None at all, and there never has been any, from the migration here till now. It has not been settled like the others were. There is no claustrum at the top up there." He pointed upward with his right hand.

"Why did the Red Hats not build up there as elsewhere?" asked Yie, puzzled by this anomaly in the general picture that he expected.

Gev seemed to look away from his two companions.

"It is hard to say, because nothing about that absence is mentioned in any books. But the Calderi have legends that cannot be substantiated."

"What do these tales hold?" persisted Yie.

"That our ancestors came here first, before the Red Hats. And when the others arrived to try to occupy and build at the summit they discovered that the area was difficult and inhospitable. In other words, they decided that other mountains were more favorable for their plans and purposes. So, the Red Hats stayed away from here. It was their own decision. They considered it better to live elsewhere.

"For some unfathomable reason, they dared not construct a colony high up on the particular peak of Calderia. The reason has always remained a mystery, though."

"I believe this is a very exceptional mountain," concluded the younger man.

"Yes," seconded Gev. "It is a special place."

The hoop wagon stopped at the foot of Calderia. Gev informed his associates that they were about to spend the night in the wood-carving dorp of Caed before pressing on the next day to the caves that were their destination.

The trio entered the village on foot with lanterns, the tinker leading them to the cottage of a woodworking artisan named Ling. The latter turned out to be a skinny, gangling elderly man with shaggy white locks and amber eyes.

"Like my ancestors for countless millennia, I have been a carver of wood all my life," said the dorper, leading Gev and the two fugitives to the mouth of the cave where the workers of his guild made and stored their products and creations.

Carrying a lantern, he took his friend and the strangers on a tour of the underground shop where the wood crafts were carried on.

Ling pointed out the hand tools lying on tables, naming each variety.

All sorts of chisels and gouges, as well as burnishers, stipplers, burins, and gravers were there. He explained in detail the specific use of each one of these.

"Most of our products are sold to the claustra on the mountain peaks," he explained. "The finest, most detailed carvings go into furniture, utensils, and decorations for the Red Hats. They collect and use our products in their mountain roosts up above us. We live on whatever they choose to pay us."

He took them on a survey of dress boxes, clothing chests, bed ends, reading desks, armchairs, cupboards, drinking cylixes, head rests, panel seats, and treasure holders.

"No dorps can afford these expensive articles," he grumbled. "Only the smallest and cheapest items go into the homes of belowers, except in the towns. These, of course, are few and quite distant from each other.

So, we are forced to depend on Red Hats as our big customers. Only they have enough sheqels to make purchases. They end up the owners of most of our wares."

They proceeded into a huge back chamber where a few mosaics and friezes of wood were being carved for specific claustra that had ordered them.

"Notice the rich floral and geometric designs of the ancestral tablets," he pointed out. Flowers, birds, animals, clouds, and even insects were visible in the carved wood. Ancestral masks revealed the faces of hegumens who had died over many generations. Everything was smooth and precise, made by able hands and sharp minds.

"Look at that expensive trigraph," muttered Ling. "It represents the Tree of Life, which for most claustra means the peach and the tree that bears it. Red Hat teachings hold that the sacred tree ripens once every three thousand years, and that whoever eats it will enjoy immortality. The peach holds the secret of escaping death. The Red Hats hold it in nearly holy status. They believe in its miraculous qualities and power.

"It was ordered by the Hegumen of Zeviv Mountain, and should be ready for delivery in the next few years. His hope is to see it installed in the hegumenia of his claustrum before his own personal demise."

Yie could not help glancing at Joa, who appeared on the verge of fainting away from what she had heard at the end.

"You must come to my cottage for evening repast," said Ling, smiling at the two visitors accompanying Gev. "We can talk more as we eat."

Roasted leporine with greengage plums comprised the supper meal provided them.

Joa and Yie, for the most part, kept silent and listened to Ling and Gev talking together. Neither one of them wished to reveal where they came from.

But as the wood carver and the tinker conversed, the pair of outsiders did not, at first, have an easy time following what they were talking about. It seemed to them an exchange between foreigners.

"Our new baaser is not at all what we thought he would be," declared Ling, his face contorted with bitterness. "Not at all. A huge disappointment."

"But he comes from among the Lingari. His ancestors were always leading carvers. Are you telling me that you woodcutters have not gotten what was hoped for from the man called Caph?"

"Careful, conservative policies are what all of us receive from him, whether Lingari, Caldari, or Rudari. No one is satisfied with this politician, no one. He fears not keeping the Red Hats happy. Therefore the concessions to the claustra continue, on and on without end. We are the servants, they are our masters."

"Aren't you exaggerating the man's faults, Ling?"

"Not at all. He is placing us so low before the highlanders that I fear some day becoming an abject slave. We sink lower and lower. No one has any hope for better conditions to come. There is despair and desperation everywhere.

"The workers of Calderia Mountain will not accept total subjugation, believe me. They would surely rise up and revolt against it. They are not people to accept oppression passively, supinely."

"They will rise up? And who do you expect will lead them, Baaser Caph?"

Gev made an attempt to laugh at this, but barely succeeded.

"Patience is what the times call for, Ling. But also silent strength and solid fortitude. We must gather together our potential power. I am certain that most of the wrongs we suffer can be righted. Caph must negotiate better prices with the Red Hats. Our standing and income must be improved, for every one of us."

"I hope to live so long," sighed the carver with a hint of cynicism.

It was time to change the subject, both of the friends agreed.

"When do you plan to go on the road again, Gev?" asked the host of the evening.

"That is still to be decided." He looked sideways at Joa and Yie. "First of all, I have certain questions to settle concerning our two friends. Where shall they live and what shall they do? I had best make an appointment to see the baaser as soon as I possibly can. He is the only one who has the authority to decide their future here. I must inform him of their terrible plight. Terrible danger hangs over them and their future. They exist in constant peril."

Ling smiled at Yie, then at Joa.

"Good luck to both of you. It is something the two of you will need."

Chapter IV

The pair in flight woke up in the hoop wagon while it was still pitch dark, hours before the heliac was due to bring brief daylight. Like all people in the belowlands, the bulk of their waking hours had to be spent in some variety of darkness. That was the major factor of life in the valleys. It determined what could be done.

Joa was quickly learning how the inhabitants of the lowlands balanced long periods of darkness with the few heliac hours that Tegumen made available for them. She realized how necessary it was for her to adjust to this pattern of living so new to her. This was not at all an easy thing to do.

Yie spoke in a worried, troubled tone to his companion.

"I have to inspect these cave facilities in order to estimate what their productive possibilities are. So far, it is only an uninformed hope I have that the needed equipment can be created here. All there is to go by are the antique drawings and illustrations in the early folios that I came upon in the depository. They may prove useful, if I can accomplish what I have in mind.

"In the final analysis, though, it may prove impossible to duplicate what was planned by the first pioneers to our planet. It is hard to visualize why they themselves failed to construct a system of complete lighting and energy for the deep valleys of this world of ours. We depend upon oil lanterns and muscle power, for the most part. Not much can be produced under these conditions, not much at all."

Joa thought of an answer to him. "Perhaps it all resulted out of fear," she told him.

"Fear?"

"The Red Hats have dreaded loss of dominance over the Yellow Hat population that settled in the lower elevations. Therefore, they deprived them of the use of iotic power. The purpose was to keep the belowers weak and helpless."

"I hate to think that was the reason for abandoning technical advances," frowned her companion in flight.

"So do I, Yie," she said, feeling a sense of shame over what her ancestors had done eons ago to subjugate the inhabitants of the valleys.

The two of them were interrupted by the return of Gev, the Tinker.

"Get up, my friends. Today we climb up to a smaller cave where iron and tin are produced from mountain ores. There is a lot for the two of you to see up there. Let's start ascending at once. We have no time to lose."

Nomb Aacn could count on the fingers of one of his hands the number of times in his long life he had come down into the valley zone of Tegumen. He remembered how unnaturally strange the land below had always seemed to him, so unfamiliar and dangerous. Now, as he met with his Red Hat cohorts in Canara, the Hegumen had a choking sensation in his throat, feeling a strangling closeness in the denser atmosphere far below the mountain summits he was familiar with.

"So, we have some information at last?" he managed to say, glaring at the subordinates assembled about him in the dorp schoolhouse that the Brothers had taken over for their own use.

One of the pursuers elected himself group spokesman and gave a report.

"Yes, we succeeded in convincing a drunken dorper to talk."

"What was it that you learned?" impatiently commanded the Hegumen.

"The pair we are seeking are continually moving about, making it very difficult to locate or follow them. They have united with a peregrinating tinker, who takes them here and there with him. Their mobility has made them nearly impossible to find or capture. They slip around as they wish. There is no clear, defined route that we can follow."

"Can't we set up a trap for them somewhere, at a spot where we think they will soon be passing by?"

"That is an almost impossible thing to anticipate, sir, except for one specific location that we are certain they will reach. It is the central depot where all these tinkers obtain their wares. It is the hub of their lives for them."

The Hegumen, growing excited, began pacing past his investigators.

"Do we have any idea where they may be?" he demanded, his voice sharp and harsh.

"Caldaria Mountain, sir," said the subordinate, trembling a little.

"Send Brothers there at once to learn if they are concealed anywhere in that area," ordered the Hegumen. "Such a place may be where I shall finally find my lost daughter and the criminal who abducted her from me."

Gev led his two traveling associates up a steep, inclined beaten path to a level ridge, then up a second hill to a hidden mountain fold. Whiffs of dark smoke came out of holes in the ground, as if from the mountain's interior.

"We must descend by steps built into the soil down to the forges below," said the tinker, pointing to a large round hole visible in the grass.

The cavern was a dark region lit by the several incandescent fires within the furnaces. The shapes rushing about to service them looked like dark ghosts of some sort, slaves to some burning divinity within the forges. The sight was an uncanny one. It made the refugees feel lost and disoriented.

Gev gave an explanation of the internal process of production going on.

"Wood charcoal is mixed with ore from a mine higher up the mountain," he told the fugitives. "The heat goes on for hours at a high intensity. Every so often, whenever needed, more fuel is added. A great blast of air is propelled into the furnace using the bellows you see on the side, keeping the temperature of the fire as high as possible. That is a necessity in order for the whole process to be completed with success.

"The ore will become like a sponge made of molten metal. The charcoal ash and the clay of the ore will form a slag that will seep through the sponge and protect the newly produced iron from chemical change of any kind.

"When the operation appears to be finished, the furnace door will be opened and the glowing ball of iron pulled out. While it is still white hot, the forgers can hammer the mass so as to expel most of the slag and shape the malleable metal into whatever form is desired.

"If we wait a little, we can see this done at once at the furnaces ready to be emptied out. It is fascinating to watch and observe. The spectacle is an impressive one indeed."

"Then, you will have a wrought form of iron," surmised Yie, smiling.

"Correct," grinned Gev. "Now, let me show you the tin forges down at the other end of the cave. I believe they will be of great interest to you."

It was Yie who was next to speak, asking a question.

"What are the metals smelted at this end?"

"Several. For instance, copper and tin are combined into bronze."

Into the mind of Yie flashed what he had read in the depository documents at Zeviv Claustrum about metals on Tegumen.

"That is interesting. But I wonder about one thing: do the metalworkers here have the capability of producing alloys with silver?"

"Silver? It is not too available. What were you thinking of as the other metal to be alloyed with silver?"

Yie, with some trepidation, gave the answer sought for. "Platinum," he whispered in a cautious tone.

Gev had no ready reply to this.

"That is hard to give an answer to. As far as I know, those two metals have never been combined much, mainly because there is no demand for it. I could also say there is no need for it, not within my memory.

"It is something of a riddle that you have asked me to answer."

Yie suddenly turned silent, saying no more at that moment.

Then Gev led the two out of the cave, back down to his hoop wagon.

Chapter V

Caph Dirua was the largest man ever to hold the office of baaser on Caldaria Mountain. He was a true giant in height, body mass, and physical domination over others. No predecessor had before reached such dimensions. Everything about him was gigantic in size.

His brownish green eyes had an almost hypnotic spell to them.

It was not until after the setting of the heliac that the two newcomers had their first opportunity to see and talk with him.

The community leader appeared unexpectedly at the hoop wagon, surprising all three who had recently arrived from off the road. Their surprise could not be concealed. It was instant.

"Gev!" shouted Caph. "I'm happy to see you back. Word reached me that there were visitors with you. I climbed down to see and meet these people."

After shaking hands with the baaser, Gev introduced him to his traveling companions. Both Yie and Joa exchanged nods of recognition with the colossal authority-holder of the metal-working community.

The latter turned to Gev with a question.

"How did the work go on your circuit this time?"

"Not badly at all. But there was one trouble that I had to deal with. It has to do with the Red Hat problem and how those haughty aristocrats come down from their eeries in the sky to abuse and mistreat all the belowers who stand in their way."

Caph wrinkled his wide brow. "What are the specifics?" he asked.

"It is not that they are oppressing me as much as the way that Red Hats are persecuting these two friends. They are the ones who have suffered."

Gev glanced a second at Yie and Joa, then faced the baaser again.

"The story is an extremely tragic one," he explained. "I will let them relate it to you in their own words."

Before Yie could begin, though, Joa seized the opportunity to give an account of her own personal history.

"I myself am a highlander, a daughter of the Hegumen of Zeviv Claustrum. Why was it that I had to take to the road? My father made himself tyrannical in every way, interfering with my most personal emotions and aspirations. In other words, he expelled my closest friend for manifesting affection toward me. I could not permit such a forced separation at all. No, I had to make my escape from the impossible situation within the claustrum.

"So, when he was thrown out, I accompanied him. There was no acceptable alternative for me. My life would have been a ruined disaster had I stayed there on the mountain, at the claustrum. It became necessary for me to leave the place along with him.

"The Red Hats decided to pursue us after we left together. They hunted everywhere, followed every possible path. Our chances appeared to be dim. But Gev took us into his wagon and brought us to this wonderful refuge, for which we will forever be thankful to him for his generous kindness."

She turned to the tinker with a glowing smile.

At the same time, Caph directed a question to the until then silent Yie.

"You were one of the Brothers on Zeviv Mountain?"

"No, not a Brother. I am a person of valley origin, an orphan from the dorp of Canara. My aunt and uncle were the ones raising me, but then I agreed to go up the mountain to become a prentice in the technical area of energy dynamics. It was while studying galactic radiation that I came across historical sources in the claustrum depository of documents that reveal aspects of science long suppressed by the Red Hats. There are certain devices and processes that could be of enormous benefit to all valley people throughout Tegumen. But they have been buried in secrecy since the original colonization of our planet so many ages ago. There had been a conscious suppression of a technology that would have saved and rescued the inhabitants of our planet's valleys. This has been the central factor in the repression and oppression of the people living in the valleys of Tegumen."

Yie paused for a moment, the baaser waiting breathlessly for him to proceed.

"It is our great good fortune that Gev has brought us to Caldaria Mountain, where belowers have the opportunity to work in metal, where knowledge of craftsmen is so much further advanced than elsewhere.

"What I propose to do is this: apply the knowledge I gained from antique documents long hidden in order to provide all belowers everywhere with a source of energy and lighting that they have never had. That is my life's supreme goal at this moment of time. That is the goal that I seek with all that is in me.

"I have committed to memory an ages-old plan to harness the rays of the heliac sun in the service of people at the low altitudes, in the valleys."

Caph, a dumbfounded expression on his face, gaped in wonder for a few moments. But then he drew himself together and asked a question that was important to him and his self-interest.

"Not only Zeviv, but all the claustra would be opposed to any such project. What sacrifices they would be willing to make in order to counter such a threat! For it is certain that they would see the success of that kind of venture as a danger to the continued survival of their primacy on Tegumen. I have no doubts that as soon as they learned of your plan, they decided to follow you with all their weapons in order to kill that enterprise in the bud. Am I not correct about that?"

"But complete silence and secrecy on our part can protect the plan until the system becomes operable," countered Yie with rising emotion. "There is no reason for any Red Hat to know what is going on. The construction of the apparati and the machinery can be disguised as something innocent and innocuous. No one shall be given a reason to suspect or deduce what is being built by us. We saw the caves of Caldaria today. What we will be doing there can be hidden from all outside eyes. I am certain of that, sir."

Yie stared with his red brown eyes, while the baaser gazed back even harder with his brownish green ones. Finally, Caph Dirua gave his judgment on what he had just heard proposed by the fugitive.

"What you talk of promises to be a long, very complicated program. There is no reason, as far as I can see, for rushing into it at breakneck speed. No, I believe in taking the necessary time to think everything out before making such an unprecedented leap into the blue. There is much that I have to learn about the plan before giving my approval. I am not one who gambles heedlessly.

"Now, as to your status as individuals in flight, let me make the promise that I shall provide both of you full protection. There is no need to remain in a wagon. My official lodge, up near the forge cave, will be available for both of you. Gev can bring you up in the morning to see these quarters that I am offering as a facility you may share with me." He seemed to fall into deep thought, then spoke to them in a low voice.

"Many people on the mountain say among themselves that I make too many concessions to the Red Hats who come here from their claustra to give us orders on products that they need or desire. But I have always been a protector of belowers and tried to preserve our resources for a future time when we will be able to stand up against the heavy exactions that they place upon us. My loyalties have always lain on the side of the people of the valleys, believe me."

The baaser then left, not saying anything more.

Joa and Yie had much to think over and discuss between themselves.

Tomorrow they were to come under the wing of a person they did not, in reality, know at all. How great a risk were they about to undertake? What were the odds that they could survive and then succeed?

Chapter VI

The minutes of light were growing longer with each passing day of spring.

Nomb Aacn, the Hegumen, did not like spending so much time in the villages, but he had to finish what he had started. Ever since the death of his wife, Joa had been his obsession, the center of his thought. Was he a possessive father? If anyone had dared ask him, he would have denied such a charge. No, he was carrying out the duty that fell to him, the only parent Joa had left. She was his most precious tie. Why shouldn't he be the very same to her? Nomb was near the point of accusing her of filial ingratitude and disloyalty. But he loved her too deeply to go that far. If once she were back on Zevis Mountain, it was clear to him that his daughter would regain her senses and relate to him as before. The tie of ancestry would be reborn. Things would go back to how they had been before.

She was, at the core, a good and faithful daughter. An outsider had come up on the peak and seduced her innocent spirit. No guilt was attributable to her childlike personality. A pure, chaste, angelic soul had been lied to and misled. Never would her father cast any accusation in her direction. She was pure and innocent.

It was the tempter who had entranced and blinded her. A belower was the one who had drawn her away from her loving parent. He was a demonic enticer. Using some mysterious belower secret, he had held Joa in a spell she was unable to break or escape from. She was a victim without personal guilt.

His baby blue eyes scanned the mountain before him, not as tall as the one his claustrum stood on, yet still sizeable in height. It lacked the thick snow that he was familiar with. Wild bushes and reddish grass covered its slopes.

What should be the next step here? the Hegumen asked himself. How best to continue with this interminable pursuit? Was it going to be successful soon?

He had to tread with care. The objective was to separate Joa from the influence of the former prentice. But there might be great difficulty in attempting that. Who could say?

He had ridden on an equine for several days and all of his bones and muscles were extremely tired. It was best to take his rest now. A squad of Red Hats had to be sent out to reconnoiter about, looking for a trail they could follow.

Their first mission was to locate the hoop wagon in question, the one that had transported the fugitives to this region.

From there, he would take up the labor of pursuit on his own.

It was surprising to the two fugitives how spacious the lodge of the baaser was. The number of rooms and their size was on a scale matching the dimensions of gigantic Caph Dirua himself. Had all his predecessors been as large as him, or had they somehow foreseen so gargantuan a resident?

Gev left the two in the care of the giant and departed quickly.

Caph took the pair on a tour of the structure, ending at the guest quarters, where he had arranged to have a set of rooms prepared for them.

"What do you think? Do they appear comfortable enough for you?"

Yie decided to get down to the serious technical matter he had in mind without delay. It seemed an opportune moment for that.

"It is not my intention to lie here idly like a parasite. There is a way that Joa and I can be of utility to the craftsman and their families inhabiting Caldaria. But it will take a lot of labor on our part to achieve anything in the cave where metals are smelted. Achievement would not at all be easy."

The big man made a wry face.

"I surmise you are referring to the scheme to harness heliac rays."

"It is not an idle fantasy, sir," argued the house guest. "If the idea were not feasible, the Red Hats would not have suppressed it with such violent force at the time of migration and colonization. They refused to allow its benefits to be available to the valleys and the people living there. It was considered too dangerous to the interests of the Red Hats and their absolute domination.

"We will never be sure what our ancestors might have achieved if early circumstances had been different for them. That is something that no one can verify or nail down. All we know for certain is the present. But the history of Tegumen might have been completely different if heliac energy could have been harnessed and brought to the valley population, descendants of the Yellow Hats. Our ancestors would not have suffered the exploitation that befell them. They would have had the ability to resist those on the mountain tops who took command of the entire planet and oppressed those down in the lower regions.

"Yes, our lives and our history could have been entirely different if heliac power had been developed for the entire planet.

"Why do those who command the heights of Tegumen hate us and deprive us of so much? What did our ancestors do to anger them so greatly? Since the time that human beings arrived on our planet, they have been cruel and merciless in their treatment of belowers.

"No one can have any doubts of their enmity to us."

Joa suddenly interrupted him. "We must not be disagreeable, Yie. Our host must make his own decisions. I have an idea: if we are furnished with paper and stylographs, we could write and draw up all that we can remember from what we read in the Zeviv depository. Then, when that exercise is finished, our host can read it at his leisure and make an informed judgment. Isn't that reasonable and practical?"

All at once, the giant gave a broad smile. "You are the one who is wisest, young lady. Yes, indeed, that is the best course to take. The two of you shall be busy with the task of formulating the newly envisioned system. Or should I call it an idea from the faraway past that was never permitted active life? Either way, I depend on your blueprint to give me a clear conception of what it is that is being proposed that we do on Caldaria. You shall have all the time required to write out the entire system as you found it in the documents that you uncovered at Zeviv Claustrum. That is the best method I can think of for moving forward."

"Thank you, sir," said Yie as politely as he was able.

Joa also looked at their new patron with warmth in her glaucous blue eyes. She saw no need to say anything more at that time.

The Hegumen rode up to the hoop wagon accompanied by his small escort of Brothers on road equines. The noise of the hoofs aroused the owner of the vehicle. Gev jumped down from the wagon, facing the band of Red Hats.

"What is it I can help you with, honorable sirs?" he anxiously inquired of the unexpected intruders.

It was Nomb Aacn who addressed the tinker's question.

"We are hunting for an abducted young woman and the criminal who took her from my house. I am the aggrieved father and she is my daughter. Have you seen two such persons anywhere that you have visited with your wagon?"

"No, I have not," bluntly replied Gev, his hands shaking with a combination of anger and fear. He was determined to say the right thing and not raise any suspicions in the pursuers of his friends. Carefulness alone would succeed at this particular moment.

"Are you perfectly certain?" continued the man on the equine. "I have cause to think you may be hiding valuable information."

"Information? Sorry, I possess no such thing. I have not come across or observed anyone matching your description of them. If I had, surely I would remember. But I did not, of that I am absolutely sure."

For a few moments, the two glared irately at each other. Neither gave any sign of conceding anything to the other.

"I hope that you are not lying to me," warned the Hegumen. "If you are, be assured that I shall hunt you down and apply a severe punishment on your guilty head. You will not be let off easily at all."

Gev looked up at him challengingly, not giving in, not retreating.

"Peregrinators like me, sir, are under the protection of the baaser of Caldaria Mountain, both here and while we are out on the road plying our craft. I do not believe that your claustral authority extends to free citizens like me and others of my guild. No, your legal jurisdiction cannot cover or include me and my wagon. Your authority in no way applies to me. Not at all."

Boiling over with rage, the mounted Hegumen signaled his followers that it was time to ride away and leave this insolent tinker alone.

Gev watched unmovingly as the Red Hats disappeared from sight, returning the way they had come.

He had to warn his close partners to stay where they were and not venture back to where his hoop wagon was parked.

They were in danger from the vengeful parent chasing them.

He had to do what he could to prevent their capture, whatever the cost.

Chapter VII

Yie unfolded the drawings and placed them on the table. Both Joa and the baaser stood looking at them across from him.

"Here is the receptor of heliac rays, as I recall seeing it depicted in the document. It receives the emission, then redirects it to the distant position where it can be converted into an iotic form that can then be used as an energy source."

Caph stared down at the illustration. "This is all quite interesting. But how do these special panels operate that absorb the iotic factors out of the light waves from the heliac so that they can be sent to the energy converters down below? That is the main problem that I see for this plan."

Yie grinned as he gave an answer to the question.

"All that the source on Zaviv Mountain alluded to was a process called sintering. That is the sum of the information furnished from the past. But I have gone to the forgers and smelters who work in the great cave, and they think that they can devise a way of making the alloy of silver and platinum referred to in the antique document.

"As I understand their scheme, they aim to granulate both of the metals first. Then, they will heat the mixture of these two to such a high temperature that the silver will melt. It will form a kind of mortar around the still solid grains of platinum. When it hardens, the silver integument will serve as the adhesive that binds together the particles of the other metal. It will glue them together into one.

"A series of repeated heatings should make th alloy solid and compact. Hammering with heavy anvils will smooth out and flatten the combination into a useable panel that can catch the rays and their energy. Such a development should do the trick successfully."

Caph looked stupefied. "But will it be economical?" he asked.

"We will have to take the panels up to the summit of Caldaria Mountain and test them," said Yie thoughtfully. "An experiment there will have to help decide if we are deceiving ourselves or not."

The Hegumen, still on his equine, took command of the twenty similarly mounted Brothers. Facing the group, he described what was ahead for them.

"I have decided what must be done. There are not enough of us to take control of the area and search for the two we are after. So, in order to strengthen our numbers, I must appeal to the claustra on the surrounding summits. They are sure to assist us with added personnel and equines. That is their sworn duty in situations similar to the one we have before us. It is their social and moral obligation to cooperate with us.

"Then, with a large host of Red Hat Brothers, things will be set for an advance. I have no doubt but that the pair are hiding somewhere on Caldaria Mountain. It is wholly unique in not having any claustrum at its peak. The place has always been a hotbed of trouble and seditious sentiments. While we are here, it would be a good deed for the sake of posterity if we cleaned out the entire cesspool of filthy muck. That would prevent trouble in the future. What do you think of my judgment on how to proceed?"

A loud cheer of support arose from the assembly of mounted Brothers.

"Good. Let us go forth to rally as many Red Hats as possible."

One by one, the others rode off behind their commander.

Joa prepared an early breakfast for Yie and herself in the kitchen of the baaser's lodge. He had already left even earlier on an inspection up at the heights of the mountain he was the ruler of. His return was expected soon.

"Is this going to work, Yie?" she asked him once they were seated and eating oatmill flans.

"No one can say with absolute confidence, but the odds are in our favor. Why would the antique source contain untruths? Surely no one back eons ago had the objective of fooling people in the distant future. We have to accept the fact that the writer was telling the truth about this technical subject. Why would all that material have been recorded unless it was true?"

"I don't know," she admitted. "But looking at the way we live on Tegumen today, who can doubt the high degree of falsity about us on all sides?

"Before I met you, Yie, I had a bad picture in my mind of the character of belowers, all of them. Until I had contact with you, my thinking was poisoned by centuries-old prejudices general among the people at the high altitudes. Our views were the result of ancient, traditional hatred. We never questioned or doubted what we had been taught about people in the valleys.

"But it was you who proved to me how untrue these stereotyped images are. I will never accept these distortions again."

She looked at him with a visible tenderness in her glaucous eyes.

"We are so different in our experiences and upbringing, Joa," said her fellow fugitive. "Where will we settle down and live together?"

She flashed a brilliant, glowing smile at him.

"When the business with the silver-platinum plates succeeds, as it must, all the land area of Tegumen will be energized and lighted. There will not be dark valleys any more. We will have many possibilities to choose from. Life will be different for us, as for everyone else as well."

"But what if the Red Hats are not reconciled to so radical a change in the technical basis of living on this planet?"

He thought deeply for a time, then gave her his conclusion.

"It may take a long time, but some resolution has to occur. In the meantime, we must stick to our plans. The first priority will be to establish that the new system of energy can work. Once that is attained, these other matters will fall into place by themselves."

Caph Dirua arrived at his mountain residence about noon, with the heliac at the zenith of its daily climb. He clearly had important news to impart, both Joa and Yie could tell from the reddened state of his face. As he spoke, his voice grew excited.

"I wanted both of you to know something as soon as possible. It worked. Our experimental run was successful. The silver-platinum panel absorbed an incredible amount of heliac radiation and converted it into the iotic variety. There can be no question but that your document was truthful. What it said came true."

"But we must go on to the next step," noted Yie. "The transmission downward has to be attempted at once. No time must be lost."

"Of course," agreed Caph. "But we can take a moment to celebrate our initial success." He headed for a kitchen cupboard made of betulawood. "I have a decanter of oenomel stored here. This is an occasion deserving of libations for every one of us."

An exuberant, elevated spirit captured hold of the pair of fugitives and their gargantuan host.

Chapter VIII

No, it will not work if my own contingent searches the mountain named Caldaria to find Joa and her abductor. Thus calculated her father, the Hegumen of Zeviv. It would be like looking for a particular insect in the forest. But what if an army of searchers were to be mobilized? What if the forces of many claustra were combined so as to trap the fugitives in a solid ring of pursuers? An army like that could form a solid net on all sides. Success would become a certainty. They would surely locate and rescue Joa.

That was the dream that drove Nomb Aacn into a frenzied visitor to as many mountain tops as he could arrive at in just a few days. He left a squad of Brothers to watch the roads from Caldaria, in case the tinker should escape with Joa and Yie. As soon as he had collected sufficient manpower, he would be able to start an effective attack on the mountain called Caldaria.

His argument grew to new, unprecedented proportions.

"We must destroy the enemy stronghold. Where else on Tegumen do the descendants of the Yellow Hats enjoy the possession of an entire mountain all to themselves? It is an unnatural condition which should never have been allowed to arise. But the time has arrived to put an end to this outrage, and we are the highlanders with the responsibility to right the wrong that exists. Am I correct about that?"

The indictment of the enemy was a bitter one, full of age-old hatred and revulsion.

"The valley farmers are nothing but ignorant peasants. What do they know? Only how to feed and reproduce themselves. Anything more than that is beyond their simple brains.

"The great problem with them is that they have never had the benefits of adequate light. That is what happened to them in both a metaphysical and a physical sense. Light alone allows ideas to form and assemble. Darkness mean separation and division for all the downlanders in the shadows. They lack the benefits of the heliac beams.

"We are fortunate that our own ancestors dwelled in the mountainous uplands. Otherwise, we might also be clods as stupid as the benighted, evil inhabitants of the low valleys.

"There are now towns and cities in the low levels. They are dark dens of crime, vice, and misery. No one in their right mind would wish to live in such hellish locations. Crowded slums, unhealthy conditions, polluted air and water, disease and epidemics prevail down there. Our mountain peaks, suffused with light, save us and our progeny from such ruinous life.

"That is the way conditions have been since the first landings on our planet. It will always remain that way, because no alternative can exist.

"Over the long ages, a better breed of people has evolved and come about on the mountain heights. The history of the valleys has been the opposite of ours. Each generation of belowers is more miserable than the ones that came before. Hatred toward highlanders grows stronger and deeper with time. There has always been great danger embodied in these miserable belowers.

"We have to maintain our superiority and control over the valleys and those who dwell there. Watchfulness on our part has become an absolute necessity. Do we wish to see our traditional system collapse? Will our descendants forgive us should we permit a catastrophe to occur? Vigilance and willingness to fight is the price of our survival and continuation. Our future is at stake every day, every hour and minute of time.

"We must combat the belowers at every turn, and never allow them to invade the mountains that are ours."

Nomb always received an answer of approval in all the claustra where he made his argument. No dissent was ever expressed. Everyone joined together in a common campaign to fulfill the goal of victory. He was successful in mobilizing the bodies and the minds of the Red Hat class in many separate locations.

He believed that victory was near, as was the return of his daughter to himself.

―――

Both Yie and Joa were busy from long before dawn until the darkness that fell after the setting of the heliac. They both remembered details they had read at the claustrum depository back at Zeviv. Most of their time was expended on the project to bring energy to the valleys through the use of the silver-platinum plates.

When will our efforts reach completion? How can we have proof whether the scheme was only someone's imagined technology or a practical invention that had been suppressed by the Red Hat authorities? Such questions dominated the thoughts of both of the fugitive lovers, becoming the obsessive concern of the couple.

Yie gave encouragement to Joa whenever she despaired, while at other times she did the same for him. She spoke to him with new conviction.

"Not until I came down below did I understand the terrible want and poverty that people of the valleys live in. At first I felt shock at these conditions. But the good character of the average belower shone through and convinced me to do what was in my grasp for the inhabitants of the lower land. And this project is the way to do that. Am I correct on that, Yie?"

He gazed tenderly at her. "You have it completely right. For me, this means repayment to those who raised and cared for an orphan all alone on our world. I am fulfilling a moral duty that I owe to the dorpers who spend more time in darkness than in the light. That is my personal purpose in all that we are doing."

She reached forward and took his larger hand in hers.

"Our effort will end in success, have no doubt about that," she murmured with confidence in her voice.

He placed his remaining hand over her hand that was clinging to his other one. "We must not let our spirits sag," he told her, his emotions passionately stirred. "I promise to give my all to the dream we share."

Gev heard the sound of hooves and awakened. Peering out of the front of his hoop wagon, he saw a sight that seemed a nightmare of the unimaginable.

A squadron of darkly dressed equine-riders surrounded him on all sides. There was no disguise that could conceal the fact of who they were. These had to be Red Hats searching for the pair he had helped elude capture. That was their reason for being there.

The tinker felt himself able and prepared to deal with these Brothers.

All I have to do is tell them part of the truth: that they are not present in the wagon. But then I have to convince these highlanders that I have no knowledge of where they may have gone. That is what I must accomplish.

Gev was confident that he could carry out such a deceptive trick. But it would take cunning and some convincing acting. Not an easy assignment at all.

One of the riders shouted at the tinker. "Get down on the ground, so that we can search the wagon. You know who it is we are after. Do not interfere with what is going to happen next."

"There is no one here at all," called out Gev as he jumped out of the front, onto a spot in front of the Red Hat addressing him.

At that moment, two riders dismounted from their equines and approached the front of the hoop wagon. They stepped forward with speed and vigor, lifting themselves up onto the front floor of the peregrinating vehicle. For them, this was difficult, serious business.

Gev turned his head to watch them rifle through his belongings. He turned back to the Red Hats' leader, whose face was hidden in murky shadow, without any individual features visible.

"Stop this criminal outrage!" he yelled out in anger. "I told you there is no one here but me. Anyone can see that, you idiot!"

"We know that," said the leader calmly. "But there could be some trace that can help us find these fugitives. Now, let me warn you about how far our search is to go.

"Unless you reveal where the two are hiding, your wagon will be set afire. These men have lucifer matches ready for that sort of task. Unless you give us the truth, it all goes up in flames. The loss will be yours to bear."

The wagon was his one and only major possession. His mind blinded by personal fury, Gev lunged forward, throwing himself onto the Red Hat who had threatened and taunted him. It proved to be the greatest mistake the tinker had ever made.

One of the Red Hats close behind the leader carried on him an antique pistolet. The weapon had apparently disappeared generations ago. There had been no need for firearms in the centuries of belower submission and passivity. Highlanders only used hunting flintlocks and muskets, nothing of such a small size. No one had developed very much skill with obsolete shooting irons like this. It had become an object with no function, no practical use.

The holder of the relic from the past did not aim with any care. His shot turned out to be a wild one. But it struck with terrible force and felled the target instantly, in a merciless, inhuman manner.

One single shot, and life fled out of the forehead of the tinker, never to return to where it had once flourished. The obsolete weapon killed the targeted craftsman.

Gev lay on the ground in front of his wagon, the first casualty of the invasion of Caldaria Mountain.

Chapter IX

Joa was first to catch sight of flames in the night.

The three individuals residing in the baaser's lodge were about to partake in a late supper meal when she happened to look out of a window facing downward to lower levels. There was no particular purpose to her act.

What she saw surprised and baffled her. What was behind these many fires? What was their meaning?

"Come over here and see something strange," she said to Yie, her voice touched with alarm.

As soon as the other saw the conflagration, he realized that the Red Hats were causing them. That was the only possible explanation. They had been located, he instantly concluded. Fire was meant to be the weapon helping to capture the two fugitives.

Caph stepped over on his own to see for himself what they were looking at so intently. He, too, recognized who was behind the disaster that was growing down below them. There could be no doubt or question about what was happening.

"What shall we do?" said Joa, sensing where the danger originated. "They will before long advance toward us."

"There is only one way off Caldaria for us. It is an obscure path that is rarely used any more. But it leads over to the other side of the mountain, then descends down into a valley so wild that no one lives there. The area is a huge hunting preserve, full of wild species of all sorts. It is an abandoned, uninhabited zone.

"There are no farming dorps there, but we can traverse that valley to reach outlying places. Once we are past the forest, we can decide in what direction to travel. It will be possible for us to chose at that time.

"It is a difficult trek, but I cannot think of any other way out that will avoid the attackers. It is our only possible safe escape route."

"Let's take it, then," said Yie with resolution in his voice.

"Yes, at once," seconded Joa.

"We cannot take anything with us if we wish to make good time. We have to leave everything behind. There is no other way."

Does that includes the silver-platinum plates, ruefully wondered Yie.

He decided to argue for taking at least two or three of them along with them in their flight.

"We must not abandon all of these promising objects," he retorted. "I think it possible to take a minimum of the plates with us. We will be sorry if we give up the hope and the promise that they represent."

The baser agreed to have his assistants carry three of the silver platinum plates with them.

The two household helpers of the baaser accompanied their leader and his two guests on their midnight journey, first on a level route to the opposite side of Caldaria Mountain, then downward into the overgrown greenery of an untamed valley where only animals could be found.

Their progress forward was slow and careful because of the lack of visibility. Caph decided that he would lead the way in a single file procession. He carried a small portable lantern that could not be seen or followed from any great distance. Step by step, the small parade moved farther away from the lodge and the approaching mounted Red Hats. Every individual recognized the danger they faced.

No one said a word until the group was on the far side of Caldaria, opposite the building they had stayed in.

The baaser raised a hand and halted, then turned around to face the others in the group.

"Time for a rest," he whispered to all those behind him.

Yie and Joa moved closer, crouching down where Caph sat.

The leader of the escape party looked at them with a confident grin on his face, as if he were eager to encourage his companions forward.

"For a short while, we will have to pass through this area of chevrotains, guars, serows, tahrs, and wild pigs. It will be a tiring effort, but there is no alternative to it. That alone is left for us.

"I have thought and thought about where we should head once we get beyond the valley on the side where there are no dorps and no people. My final opinion must be this: the safest place has to be a town. The Red Hats will not be able to trail us there. The closest such municipality is the one called Rocumbol. I myself have never been to the town, but we are certain to find protective shelter there. The townsmen come from the same origins that we do, the Yellow Hats of old. Common ancestry must be the bond that ties us to them and vice versa."

"Is there any degree of risk involved for Yie and me?" inquired Joa with a definite amount of anxiety in her voice. "My fear is that there could be a traitorous informer, even within a town. What if someone reports our presence to those pursuing us?"

Caph thought for a moment, then gave his considered view.

"Yes, there exists some risk, but the much greater danger is not to enter Rocumbol. We will have to hunt for friendly supporters and place our trust in them. My plan is not a perfect one, yet is there any other way out for us? Can anyone think of some other destination for us to choose?"

Neither of the fugitives made any response to that.

Was there any questioning of the fact that the Red Hats had brought about the ruin of the heliac energy project?

How would it be possible to reinstitute the experimental achievements already carried out on Caldaria? They were surely not going to be easy to continue.

The silver-platinum plates were mostly left behind, apparently never to be retrieved. There was no chance of going back for them. The three carried with them held little chance of successful use.

The trek started again as Caph picked up his lantern and signaled to the others to follow him into the long night.

Dayspring, as always, arrived late in the valley on the far side of Cadaria Mountain.

The party of five was descending slowly into the dark green forest. The leader, Caph, motioned to the others to stop for a rest. From below came the bell sounds of campanero birds. The baaser, Joa, and the two helpers sat down, but Yie still stood. Something was troubling his mind and now was the moment to express what it was.

"I must go back," he unexpectedly said, his reddish brown eyes focused on the leader from Caldaria. "The rest of the heliac plates must not be left on the summit of the mountain. We must bring them along with us. They hold the future of our planet and will determine what life will be like in the future."

"But think of how heavy they are," objected Caph. "It would be much too difficult. Think of the danger from the Red Hats we would be exposing ourselves to. How could we ever expect to succeed?"

"I am willing to go back myself for them," asserted Yie. "They must be preserved and used again. The dream of power for the valleys must not be permitted to die. It must never be surrendered, not by us."

The baaser thought a couple of seconds.

"We can go on to Rocumbol and hire a gyag. Joa can remain there at an inn while we return to rescue the remaining plates. Then the transport of the heavy objects could turn out to be feasible. Does that make sense to you, Yie?"

The latter nodded that it did.

Soon they began walking again with newborn hope within them.

The silver-platinum plates would continue to hold their dream of light and energy for the valleys of Tegumen. But they had had to leave the bulk of them back on Caldaria Mountain.

Chapter X

Yie began to see with his mind's eye, independently of specific time or location. His thoughts took leaps and journeys to other sites and occasions, as if there were no physical or temporal limitations or laws. He knew, at the last moment, that what he experienced were products of imagination. That did not stop him from proceeding with the series of ideas that seemed to come to him from nowhere specific.

Where was he? In the past or in the future? On what part of the planet?

A new Tegumen existed, unlike the one he knew, with villages and mountains of old. A different world with a different way of living. Nothing familiar, nothing like what he knew from his own life. The past no longer held sway, as if it had never existed. Everything was entirely changed.

Light and motion, prosperity and happiness, invention and enlightenment. A life unlike what anyone alive had ever seen. Unlike what Yie himself had imagined possible. This was an environment whose nature was not the one that existed. Was it the future to come? Or was the picture one of a past that might have been, but never was back then at all? Was it a lost opportunity, a repressed alternative? A world never attained, now totally impossible?

There was no way to answer such questions, at least till the vision became reality.

The fleeing group came into a short, narrow vale with towering ridges on all sides. There was only a dim, twilight light about.

"We shall be stopping at the dorp called Molina," indicated Caph, pointing downward at the stone mill where local cereals were turned into flour. "I am acquainted with the miller who owns and operates that important enterprise. His name is Bie. I am sure that he will be happy to accommodate us so we can rest before making the last leg of the journey to Rocumbol."

The miller, a heavy-set, gray-haired man up in years yet possessing the vigor and strength of a youth, greeted Caph and his companions with warm, friendly greetings and smiles. He led the travelers into his small cottage beside the grinding mill and the river that it used for power.

The group seated itself in the tiny spence in the front of the home of the most prosperous person in Molina. Simple padded squabs were the furniture upon which the tired walkers rested themselves. They were too exhausted to proceed onward any further. Rest had become necessary.

The wife of Bie served tiny plates containing secale turnovers full of mountain baiberries. She followed this with cups of piping warm anthemis tea from field herbs. All the visitors enjoyed the taste of the harmonious combinations of flavors. Caph complimented the housewife on her fine food and drink, while she and her husband grinned their thanks in return.

Bie expressed what was on his mind.

"It is no secret to the people of Molina Valley what happened on your mountain when the Red Hats made their terrible attack. How immoral and shameless these people are! I hope that some day these particular malefactors receive fitting punishment for their crimes. But who will make them pay the price for these unjust deeds?"

Caph took up the conversation from that point on.

"We must make it to Rocumbol as fast as possible," he stated, changing the subject a small degree. "Where else can we go to hide? What other long-term refuge is there for us?"

He exchanged searching looks with the muscular, aging miller.

"I wish that our dorpers could help you more, but you can see what our condition has fallen to. The Red Hats come here and impose their exactions of taxes and rent, until only the minimum necessary for survival is left us. Nothing more, beyond a few things like you just tasted yourselves.

"Like most of the dorf inhabitants of our region, we are not connected to any cables that could bring a small amount of iotic energy down from the mountain claustrum that exercises socage jurisdiction over us. We must climb up a mountain to a highlander court in order to sue for justice if we have any claims or disputes to decide.

"Our education is extremely meager, for we have only limited schools that lack adequate teachers.

"So it is a plain, hard life that is lived in Molina. I know, for I mill the small harvest that each cultivator is able to raise. Our fields are small, situated where the mountains permit a few extra minutes of heliac light each day. Most of our valley territory is at an improper, indirect angle, not adequate for full cultivation of a crop. Any crop.

"What do our people grow? A poor trigo grain, from which an insufficient farina flour is produced in my mill. And our seigle turns into an inferior type of rye grain. No, our inhabitants must also turn to hillside herding of sheep, because agriculture of any kind is too difficult to sustain a belower family by itself.

"And this has been the condition of our valley for countless centenaries of time. It goes on that way forever, without change or improvement of any kind."

Caph, all of a sudden, made an audible grumbling sound.

"It is the same everywhere on Tegumen, a planet where only the highland mountain peaks are able to thrive, not because of what they produce, but because they take with impunity from the rest of the population, those below them in both altitude and social rank. That is our history, unchangeable down to today. The course of our lives has been one of misery and hopelessness."

Unexpectedly, Yie interrupted him with his own view of the future.

"For me, that picture of oppression cannot and will not last forever. My hope is that the system can be turned upside down and shaped into something different."

Bie grew excited upon hearing this statement.

"How is change to be brought about?" he inquired with desperation in his voice. "What is the means by which we can achieve what we aspire to? Can anything be done after centuries of oppression and exploitation?"

It was not Yie but Caph who supplied an answer.

"So far, we have only prospective ideas. New technology and inventions are the central part of what will be needed. If we are able to change how belowers live and work, the old ways of the planet will have to be replaced by fairer, juster methods. That is the hope that keeps us in the battle for what will be."

The exchange of views appeared to reach an end by itself, with everything of importance said in as much as it had any practical importance.

That night the fugitives slept on cots brought to the grain mill by dorpers.

Early the following morning, the trekkers departed with the best wishes of Bie and the inhabitants of Molina.

Part 3

Chapter I

Rocumbol lay in a deep fold between soaring overhead peaks. Its evolution into a city was gradual, almost unperceived by the oldest inhabitants. Tools, implements, and utensils for the lowland population of the nearby and distant valleys were the objects of its crafts and industries. Trade and exchange, though, were the lifeblood of Rocumbol. Without commerce, there would be little to draw country people to its cobbled streets of stone and brick.

Coal gas lanterns lit the streets both at night and through dim daylight. Work went on in its shops and factories from darkness to darkess, through the three or so hours of twilight illumination from the sky. There seemed to be a permanent cloud of mental depression to accompany the short, shadowy period labeled day. Rocumbol had an atmosphere of murk and shade that no one could overcome and defeated everyone. There was nothing of a happy nature in the daily life of the urban residents. Darkness characterized both the material and psychological levels of existence here.

The baaser found an inn where he and his companions could stay. He paid for two rooms, one for Joa and the second for himself and Yie. The decision was to keep the several silver platinum plates concealed behind a large dresser in the latter. After a full supper of roast carnero, greens, and carnotes, the three took a walk through the narrow oil-lit streets of central Rocumbol. No one said anything as the baaser led the other two onward. He had said nothing when they were eating. Had he some specific destination in mind tonight? wondered both Yie and Joa.

All at once, the leader stopped. They stood before an overhead sign that read "Popular Theater".

"This is where I aim to look up an acquaintance of mine," he explained with a grin. "His name is Frelo, and he is director of the drama establishment that you see. Come, I will buy us tickets and we will go in to see his current production. It is certain to take our minds off our current troubles and worries."

The presentation for that evening, an historical play about pioneering migrants on the planet, had already begun. The first act was about to finish as the three sat down in the back of the darkened auditorium. Only a dozen or so people made up the diminutive audience for the stage production then in progress. They were a noiseless, soundless group that never made any comment.

It was easy for the newcomers to pick up the thread of the thin plotline of the drama in progress.

Hardy agriculturists were being compelled to turn to mouflon herding because of the poor growing conditions of the valleys. Conflict with highlanders occurred over mountain law claims and boundaries. The hero and the heroine were strangers, kept apart by narrow, frugal parents on both sides. But love triumphed when the protagonist succeeds in amassing the largest herd of animals in his dorp. The lovers united in formal wedlock performed by a friendly blamus, yet the valley was still left wallowing in miserable poverty. The perpetual hardness of life was only temporarily forgotten in the bliss of mating. A sad, bittersweet ending came at last, in the last act of the performance. The drama ended on a note of despair.

As soon as the play was over, the public in the theater seemed to flee outside. No applause greeted the actors on stage. They disappeared in the flash of an eye, as did the viewers of the presentation. The end seemed total and swift.

The baaser rose and turned to his two companions.

"Follow me," he whispered. "We are going backstage."

Not knowing what to expect, Yie and Joa did as he told them to.

He seemed well acquainted with the lay-out of the theater, taking them along a side aisle to a rear corridor with a series of closed dressing rooms.

A tall man in charge of scenery and props came up to the baaser. The pair exchanged a few words. "Frelo is in the office at the end," said the theatrical producer, pointing down the hallway at a dark, recessed door.

The baaser proceeded onward, the two others in tow.

A single knock on the indicated door was followed by "Come in."

Into the office entered the threesome as a unit.

A short man with tiny arms and feet sat at a small desk. His gray hair was outshone by argent eyes. The sharpness of the latter indicated a lively, comprehending mind behind them.

Frelo recognized at once the man at the head of the grouping. He rose from his chair with gusto. Without a word of greeting, he embraced the baaser as best he could. But the silver eyes then took in the two standing behind his friend.

"These are close associates of mine who escaped Caldaria with me. You have heard of the shameless assault that we suffered?"

"Only the general outline," answered Frelo, rising to his feet. He shook the hand of first Joa, then Yie.

"Both of you have my sincerest sympathy," muttered the director of the Popular Theater. "All my heart goes with your sufferings."

"Let me give you the specifics of what occurred," said the baaser. "It is an extremely tragic story."

Frelo bit his thin lower lip. "This building will soon be closed. All of you must come with me to my apartment. There we will have an opportunity to go into all these matters at some length."

In a short while, the four of them departed from the theater.

Frelo lived alone in a flat over a furniture and furnishings store.

He seated himself beside the baaser on a plain chair, facing a love seat where Joa and Yie situated themselves.

After offering his guests gateaux and crackers, the little impresario got down to the subject that most interested him.

"Shall we let our mortal enemies enjoy victory after victory? Can we never put a halt to their attacks and predations upon our people? How much longer must we suffer before we gain some relief? My mind and my heart have been torn to pieces by the news about what the Red Hats did in recent days."

The baaser answered him. "We must never forget the record of their crimes. Let me relate the recent history that our mountain went through."

For the next several minutes, Frelo listened with patience and attention to the specific details presented to him. With enormous effort, he held in check his mounting indignation. Only when the baaser finished, did the director give expression to the anger he had been stifling inside himself.

"This is outrageous. Intolerable. Why must the suffering, the inhuman pain continue on and on? When will delivery and liberation arrive for us? The pain suffered by our belowers never reaches any kind of end."

He gazed first at Yie, then Joa. It was the latter who gave a reply.

"The advantage that the highlands have is simply their abundance of light and galactic energy. And that is the great deficiency down here below. Is that to be the permanent fate of the oppressed population of the lowlands?"

Frelo suddenly seemed to become distant and abstracted.

"I have always tried to utilize theatrical drama to remind our inhabitants of the yoke they dwell under. Traditional comedy makes fun of the conventicles, poking at their vanities and foibles. Romantic tragedy shows how even individual, private lives are affected by their interference and exploitation of us. Again and again, I have attempted to bring to the audience a conscious realization of our ancient plight. We are the low ones and our enemies live up on high, far above. That is the continuing truth. That is the foundation of all our personal misery and unhappiness.

"I have tried to keep burning the flame of just resistance. It has been difficult. Popular taste often seeks diversion and excitement. In other words, idle escape. But that has never been my purpose in presenting these dramatic shows."

A thoughtful silence came over all four of them.

All at once, Yie found himself making a proposal to the director, one that surprised even himself as he listened to it.

"We need an active enterprise of some sort. Of any kind, to be accurate. I do not believe any of us have knowledge or experience with drama or the theater. But that may turn out to have advantage in what I think we should try to put and say on the stage.

"Why not present an enactment of what happened on Caldaria? Why not reveal how the oppressors keep us from constructing means of enjoying the light and energy of the heliac? Wouldn't such a project help mobilize the citizens of this city? Give them a spirit and direction you have just told us is lacking today? The effects could be a revival and magnification of public feeling.

"I do not know how practical such a program might be. But at heart it involves positive thought and purposeful activity. It could prove to be the key that opens the door to new, previously unimagined possibilities."

Frelo held his hand under his chin, considering the unusual plan. His mind moved with lightening speed. In an instant, he knew that he had to accept this provocative project, regardless of risks and difficulties.

"I think there are useful benefits involved, though it will not at all be easy to mount. The presentation of such a play could be fruitful in many ways. With the aid of all three of you, I believe that I can compose a tentative draft in a few days. But I shall need help from all of you. Will I have it?"

"Certainly," nodded the baaser.

"Yes, of course," said Yie.

"We will do all we can," chimed in Joa.

"Let's get to work on it immediately tonight," decided Frelo, his eyes shining with new enthusiasm.

He went to a corner desk, opened a drawer, and took out a file of blank sheets and several stylographs. Returning to the others, the director distributed the paper and pens.

"Each of you can write down your primary memories of what occurred in the battle over Caldaria. That will be the raw material for the play we construct to reanimate the wrath of our public."

Chapter II

Frelo found two empty apartments near the Popular Theater for his new associates. The baaser and Yie moved into the larger and Joa took the adjacent flat.

The four acts of the play named "Caldaria" jelled into a structure with astonishing speed. A flood of excitement seized all involved in the project. There was no retreating now. This play was meant to incite and activate all who saw it. Incendiary drama was their goal. It was meant to ignite the emotions of those who would see and hear it. This was to be theater with a highly political purpose behind it.

But the enemy from the high peaks above was not absent from the narrow streets of Rocumbol. Red Hats mounted on equines, in squad formation, tramped along, frightening the belowers out of their way. Yie saw them in one twilight period, hiding himself in a shop entrance so as not to be noticed by the Brothers riding by on their animals. He only felt relief when they were gone.

Later, at the theater, he told Frelo what he had seen. The director made a wry, ironic face of dissatisfaction.

"What can we do? They cannot be stopped if they wish to enter our city. Those devils often come to take this or that from our stores and shops. Who dares to call it by its true name of shameless stealing? That is what, in reality, these riders commit. But they go home to their eeries unpunished. It would be a disaster to try to arrest them. We have to suffer whatever the Red Hats choose to do among us. There is no remedy against it."

The two went on to the stage scenario of the drama in process of creation. "I want the best possible scenery and lighting," said Frelo with emotion. "Nothing is to be omitted that can aid in presenting a realistic picture of the mountain environment. Everything must be genuine and accurate. Although gas lighting has certain negative features, they can be overcome with optical instrumentalities. I have the best theatrical lighting expert in all of Tegumen traveling here to work with us. His name is Cacque, the photist. Have you ever heard of him?"

"No," confessed Yie, his voice mild and conciliating.

"He should be in Rocumbol soon. I believe that Cacque can add a lot to the vivacity of the production. He is a superb master of his craft of stage lighting. No one else has comparable skills to his."

The baaser succeeded in his attempts to become acquainted with the most enlightened leaders of the city. In all the guild organizations of Rocumbol, he discovered young malcontents dissatisfied with the passive, timid attitude of their superiors toward the long-established system of hierarchy on Tegumen.

"Why do we allow those demonic Red Hats to walk all over us?" asked one dissident over alegar in a smoke-filled tavern.

"It is our own fault, nobody but ours," he concluded in wrath.

When asked if he had brought any answers with him from Caldaria, the newly arrived baaser gave no immediate or specific reply.

"We must be watchful and awake," he frequently told new friends. "No one can say when our salvation will arrive, though it must."

CLEMENT MASLOFF

Cacque was a huge figure, heavy in weight with enormous, muscular arms and legs. Curly auburn hair enclosed a circular face with dull gray, galenic eyes. For all his size, he moved himself about with surprising speed and dexterity.

There was something impressive and attractive about him.

Both his mother and father had been actors of a roaming troop of players. Throughout Tegumen, the child had traveled with parents, becoming familiar from the inside with the arts and crafts of the temporary theaters. Nothing surprised this expert in drama presentation. He possessed familiarity with every aspect of the profession he had inherited.

It was in his teen years that the young Cacque decided to train himself in the scenery and illumination of plays. It was not a result of his lack of the gift for acting. He had the inner character of both parents, yet was without the necessary ambition to be a center of stage attention. In an odd way, his interest in the minutia of theater technology drew him away from the ordinary dreams of stage stardom and prominence. Few could compare to Cacque in detailed knowledge of how to present plays. His artistic skills had to do with the physical surroundings of the actors and their roles.

The huge young man came directly to the Popular Theater as soon as he arrived in Rocumbol. He found Frelo, an intimate friend for years, in his office at the theater. The two men, laughing with joy, embraced as they greeted each other. Memories of past dramatic successes arose in both of their minds. They felt deep. powerful nostalgia.

When they were seated, the director began describing the new play that he planned to put on the stage that he managed.

"It is a story of oppression and resistance. A terrible conflict is fought for control of the mines and forges of Caldaria. That will be the title of the play: "Caldaria". It will have a profound meaning for every belower who witnesses it. The theme has power to touch and melt many hearts. My purpose is to try to ignite a sense of the possibilities ahead for the people around us, despite the bitter experiences of loss and defeat they have gone through."

The two old friends stared at each other for a time.

"Three refugees from the invasion of Caldaria are here in Rocumbol, assisting me with their stories. In fact, they are providing narratives of the incidents that occurred and writing authentic dialogue for the play. I imagine that you want to meet them as soon as you can." He rose to his feet. "Let me take you to the apartments they occupy. It is only a short walk there."

Cacque, curious to see the strangers, stood up. "Yes, let me meet and talk to these fugitives from the Red Hats."

Five persons congregated about the table in the dining room of the apartment shared by Yie and the baaser. After making introductions for the benefit of Cacque, Frelo gave a synopsis of the projected production he planned to present to the public at the Popular Theater.

"The central theme, of course, is the conflict with the highlanders. Their oppressive domination over our existence should be evident to each and every member of the audience. The Red Hats block all attempts to restore our mines and forges on Caldaria. Failing to intimidate the metallic craftsmen, they finally invade and destroy the workshops in the last act of the play. Can you make all of that graphically alive with scenic design and lighting, Cacque?"

The latter pondered for a couple of seconds before giving his opinion in a slow, reflective tone of voice.

"Yes, there are elements of the narrative that can capture the attention and emotions of the most stolid of viewers. For instance, the use of fire as a weapon by the invading Red Hats. There is room for spectacular lighting effects with that factor. I can foresee the placement of parabolic reflectors at various stage positions so that gas flame can be multiplied many times over in the separate scenic locations. The catastrophe in the last act should excite and horrify everyone in the theater with its accuracy and realism. I am certain that a dynamic cyclorama can be built that reaches a height of impression and influence. All my creative experience will be focused on making the scenes as truthful and emotionally powerful as possible. I promise that to all of you, as both an artist and a belower. Nothing less than the best will I try to create for this special project."

The eyes of the four others centered upon him.

"Our play depends on its ability to seize hold of the minds viewing it," quietly said the director, Frelo. "This drama will be our spark, aimed at producing a conflagration inside many minds. We must rise to the opportunity of the occasion, all of us. You speak of a cyclorama, Cacque. We have in Rocumbol never applied such an advanced method on any stage. But I have heard and read of it. Could you explain it for all of us?"

The scene designer smiled. "Of course. It is a device to create the illusion of spatial depth on stage. I have built a number of them at various theaters in the cities of Tegumen. What it consists of is a large cylinder of canvas cloth laced onto two semicircular iron pipes, above and below. It is illuminated from overhead and below by gas burners with parabolic reflectors about them and chromatic prisms over the flames. These prisms are very accurately and delicately calibrated to break down and recombine the gas light. Red, blue, and green are refined, then compounded and combined again. The intensity of each light can be controlled by switches so as to produce desired effects on the cloth of the cyclorama. As a result of all this, the color of the whole scene can be changed through the entire range of the spectrum. There is no limit to the variety of chromatic combinations attainable. The effects can be astounding. The audience will be fascinated by what they see on the stage.

"What I plan to construct is a cyclorama that produces the impression of the largest, most intense fire imaginable. My aim will be to terrify the audience into believing it is present at a great fire on Caldaria."

Yie immediately asked a question.

"Is there any problem of safety involved in that method?"

"I will take all steps necessary to maintain absolute control through the valve gauges. There has never been an accident in my experience with the cyclorama projections. I promise to stay vigilant at all times."

The baaser made an inquiry. "You mentioned the use of prisms. Are they large ones?"

Cacque turned to him and spoke in a low murmur.

"For several years I have worked with glass-makers at various sites to make prisms that are small and have very little weight to them. Through trial and error, we have developed better, more useful ones. Some I have ordered to be sent here to Rocumbol. But other models will have to be produced in this city. Is that feasible?"

"I believe so," answered Frelo. "We have skilled glass-blowers among us. I think that they can meet your needs, Cacique. There should be no problems in supplying the prisms. You shall have what you need to produce such a spectacle."

After more discussion of the scenic needs, the group of five left for a nearby inn to have a late meal together.

Chapter III

Nomb Aacn hated all the towns and cities of the belowers, but especially Rocumbol, the closest one to his own mountain conventicle on Zeviv.

All the reports that came to him from his mounted agents pointed to that municipality as the nest where his daughter and her lover had found refuge. Word of sightings arrived, though cloudy and indefinite. Enigmatic traces could only be examined and investigated on the spot, and only by the Hegumen himself. So, Nomb swallowed his pride in order to send an official missive written in his own hand to the city qadic of Rocumbol, the highest and most potent magistrate of the lowlander community.

"...so it is my wish to enter and stay in your city in order to carry forth a wide-ranging probe in search of a member of my family and the abductors who have carried her off. I plan to come with a contingent of Brothers on equines who will assist me in this work of hunting down and capture. We shall not interfere in any way with the normal life of Rocumbol, but shall need and appreciate the assistance of the police officials of the municipal government. I am certain that there will be full, absolute cooperation between my unit and every peace-keeping officer under your own command..."

So said the message that surprised and discomforted the qadic and his ruling council. What were they to make of this brazen intrusion? How would a large contingent of Red Hats behave once stationed in the city? How much interference with city residents was to be expected with such an unexpected invasion from the highlands? Serious problems and difficulties appeared to be coming to Rocumbol.

The qadic was a thin, scraggy man with dusky umber eyes in a pale, wrinkled face. He revealed much of his internal fear in the words he spoke to the councilors at the municipal hall.

"This is a serious matter with grave dangers in it for our city. Of course, the Hegumen must be received and furnished with official hospitality. Beyond that, every step we take has to be measured and deliberate. There must be no surrender of independence, but also no sign of opposition or resistance.

"Both you and I will have to walk a cautious, thought-out line. Our policemen shall give limited aid to the mounted Red Hats. No more than an appearance of compliance with demands and requests is necessary. I have decided upon a specific policy: our officers have to inform me of all moves by our guests. Should they pick up the trail of those they seek, you and I have to be informed instantly. We do not want a confrontation with highlanders. The best way to avoid any catastrophe will be to keep what is hidden under a cover of continuing, permanent secrecy. If the Hegumen and his Red Hats find nothing, they will have to leave eventually. But if they succeed in finding these kidnappers, there shall be nothing but trouble for our city.

"Therefore, my objective is to convince Nomb Aacn that he dominates me and my administration. As long as that illusion can be maintained, anything with the potential to disrupt the situation will remain unseen and unrecognized. Is that policy of mine acceptable to you, the city council?"

All those who heard him accepted his ambiguous, deceptive way out of the sensitive political dilemma that Rocumbol was soon to face.

Joa, after reading a handbook on drama given her by Frelo, had an idea that jolted the director. She brought it up at the Popular Theater in a discussion of the cast that was to play in the new production.

"Why have traditional actors?" she asked the group that included Yie, Caph, and Cacque. But her question was specifically aimed at Frelo.

"What are you thinking of?" asked the latter.

The eyes of the other three focused on the exchange of these two.

"From what I have learned about the history of drama, there was in earlier ages a great deal of room for on-stage improvisation. The actors possessed full freedom to add or omit lines, as each of them saw fit. In that way, no two performances were identical. The inspiration of the moment ruled and was able to insert ideas and statements where and when needed.

"I am therefore proposing that the core of our cast consist of Yie, Caph, and myself. We experienced the battle of Caldaria. Who better than the three of us to present a living re-enactment?

"My sense is that only participants like us can guarantee true authenticity."

Everyone who heard this seemed stunned for several seconds.

Caph and Yie looked at the director as if expecting him to refute the astounding claims made by their fellow refugee from Caldaria.

No response coming from the dumbfounded Frelo, Yie decided to reveal his own reaction to his lover's unanticipated proposal.

"That is a very novel idea, Joa. When did it occur to you?"

His implication was this: why did you not present it to me first, and exclusively? Why do you spring it full blown on our entire group?

She turned and looked at Yie with a beaming, radiant smile. Her voice was balanced and controlled, as if addressing a person not at all intimate.

"I know that you can accomplish it, along with Caph. We need not be golden-voiced and smooth-talking. Our advantage is the reality we can give. We were present and witnessed what the Red Hats accomplished with violence and terror."

A silence followed, for no one wished to refute her by attacking the ideas she had brought before them. None of the males had come near to imagining such a casting of the persona of the play. Her proposal had surprised them.

Finally, Frelo was the one to suggest a temporizing expedient to the group that appeared stunned and stumped.

"We are at an early stage of development," he informed them. "There are many alternatives to choose among, and that is only one of them. What I propose to do is this: use the three actual participants in our early beginning rehearsals. That will be done to see how the concept pans out on the stage. All three of you can play yourselves. Then, we can judge how it looks. And you on stage can tell me how you feel being yourselves in the play. How does that sound? Does it seem reasonable?"

No one demurring, the solution was acknowledged by all and at once accepted.

Frelo turned to Cacque and changed the topic of discussion.

"How are your lighting problems advancing?" he inquired.

"I have been visiting all the local glass-blowers. As expected, the best of them are familiar with the prisms that my theater will need. In fact, I learned that there is one person who has the ability to produce a prismoid for us."

"A what?" said Frelo with surprise.

All eyes were on the stage designer as he explained.

"There is a subtle difference in the geometry of a prism and a prismoid. Let me describe it, so we can all recognize what it is.

"In a prism, the end surfaces are polygons, equal in shape and size. The two ends are parallel. But the several sides between these ends are all parallelograms, all of them.

"But if you take a prismoid, it only resembles a true prism. The ends may be parallel to each other, but they form unequal polygons. The ends are not identical. Therefore, the sides of a prismoid are trapezoids, not parallelograms. They can never be parallelograms. Never."

Caph then asked a question. "What practical difference does that make for stage lighting, my good man?"

Cacque grinned, looking directly at the baaser.

"The light is not only magnified many times over, but its nature undergoes an unexplainable change. I cannot give any scientific explanation, but there is a transformation within a plasmoid that does not occur when one uses a simple prism such as I described for you. It has to do with the optical angles that the light corpuscles travel. I do not have any formal grounding in optics that I could apply to the production of this changed form of light, but I know how to make it happen."

All at once, Yie spoke up. "I wish that I had some of the old texts of Zevis here with me. They might contain some useful reference to prismoidal light that would help us understand it better."

Cacque gave a laugh. "The Red Hats are not ones to try out new methods in anything. We can only depend on ourselves for advancement in stage lighting. No one else will be of any help at all, I can assure you."

"Yes," admitted Yie. "Everything depends on us alone."

Chapter IV

Joa appeared taken aback by an attitude she had never before seen in the young man who had taken her from the peak of Zeviv Mountain.

"I don't understand why you did not tell me ahead of time about the proposal of yours to make actors of us. It has turned out to be something of a total surprise to me in all that it requires be done in preparation."

The two were close together, sitting in the parlor of her flat, on low placerwood stools.

"There was no need to do so," she shot back at him. "It might have made it appear that I valued your opinion more than that of anyone else involved. That could have been an impression causing problems. Don't you see that?"

"No, not at all. That is a speculative idea, nothing more," he told her with an angry expression in his voice and on his face.

It was then her turn to pose a jolting question to him.

"What would you have told me if I had revealed my idea to you first? Can you say that you would have told me to stop and forget the whole project?"

"But you did not ask for my opinion ahead of that of all the others, Joa. And I am uncertain at this moment what I might have answered. Yes, I accept the scheme sufficiently to try it out tomorrow when we rehearse for the first time. I am not an actor, but I will try to perform as one.

"I can only imagine how I might have reacted if we had been alone, not part of the full group. I can only guess at my answer, so don't ask me that again."

"Don't worry, I have no intention of asking you about things in the past," reacted Joa with a slight forced grin.

"But what happens now?" he asked her. "Will the play be a success on the stage?"

"If I have anything to do with it, we will become effective actors, both of us along with Caph. I will try the best I can on stage, Yie."

He made a sly, knowing grin, which she answered with a sudden smile of her own.

Cacique made his way through crowded, narrow ways till he came to Vitrics Lane. Here was where he planned to make contact with the best glassblower in Rocumbol. There was no way for him to know ahead of time what was possible or impossible for a master of the craft to provide him for his stage lighting. This was the day he meant to learn that by talking with a glass expert.

The scenery designer asked a youth in gray apprentice clothes who was passing for directions to the desired location.

"Can you point out the workshop of Master Dijo, please?"

"I work for him as an undergrub, at the third gate on the left side."

The young lad pointed to the place, then ambled away. Cacique hurried to the oaken gate. Day was advancing and only an hour and a half of twilight remained over the city before darkness fell again.

He knocked once, then twice, before pushing open the barrier gate. Stepping forward, the stage designer entered the small courtyard of the vitric specialist he was looking for.

A male of medium height and build approached him. There was sweat on his puffy cheeks and broad brow. The brick red face was flushed till it nearly matched the coppery eyes that were burning with flame.

"Hello, sir. Can I help you? My name is Dijo, the glass-maker. What is it you are seeking in my establishment?"

The two figures stood facing each other in silence until Cacique began by giving his name. "You cannot be familiar with me or my reputation, for I am not a native of your fine city. But I am called here to finish a task for the Popular Theater. You know where it is located? I am serving as scenery designer and that places me in charge of the gas lighting for the stage. There will be a production, very soon, that demands extremely complicated and sophisticated glasswork devices. I have been informed that you are the leader in that field and can complete very complicated orders."

"Indeed, it is no boast to tell you that I am just that."

Cacique took two steps forward, till he stood immediately in front of the master in gray work clothes and dark leather apron. "What specifically is it that the Theater needs?" the craft-master directly asked the stranger.

Cacique hesitated, holding back several seconds.

"Many are familiar with what a prism is, but I am interested in the creation of what I call a prismoid. That is what I believe that I will need."

Dijo made a sudden unconscious grimace, reflecting his confusion.

"I am sorry, you will have to define what that is for me. It is an unfamiliar term that you use. I do not have knowledge of what it means."

With a pleasant smile, the visitor proceeded to do just that.

It took him longer than he had planned, but after a minute or so signs of understanding appeared on the face of the glass-blower.

The latter began muttering in a low, questioning voice. "A prism that is cock-eyed and askew! Nobody has ever ordered such an oddity from me before. I have no actual experience to go by. But over the years orders for small prisms have come my way and I have filled them with success. With superior quality, if I say so myself."

He thought for a moment, staring intently at Cacique with cupric eyes.

"I will say this much: a try can be made on this," said the glassman. "That is all that I can honestly promise. All my knowledge and skill will go into my work. If it is at all possible, I will make it for you. But there can be no guarantees on a completely new item like this. The task will be difficult."

"That much I realize," remarked Cacique, suppressing the joy he felt. Victory was approaching, he could sense its coming.

"Bring me a drawing of exactly what you require, the dimensions, angles, and surface areas. It will take me time to figure out all the steps and the turns needed in the blowing of the glass. No, this operation will not be an easy one, not at all. What you demand will present a colossal challenge."

"I know, but the Popular Theater will reward you generously," promised the stage designer.

"Objects like an oblique prism are not created only for money," said Dijo with a wink. "This will raise my professional reputation to the sky. But I have to make the thing first. Bring me your drawings, even if it is dark outdoors. I mean to start work as soon as I can."

Dijo extended his right hand and Cacique shook it.

Until tonight, then," said the latter, heading out of the tiny courtyard.

As he returned to his flat that evening from delivering his prismoid designs to the glass-blower, Cacique heard the noise of stomping equines along the street and stepped under an overhanging dormer roof to watch a squad of mounted Red Hats go by. He gazed at the sight until they disappeared toward the center of Rocumbol, then continued toward his apartment, puzzled and confused by this sinister presence in the city.

The intruders only halted when they reached the official house inhabited by the qadic and his large family. It was here that Hegumen Nomb Aacn climbed down. One of his guards took hold of the reins of his steed. Meanwhile, the qadic exited through the front door and moved forward to greet and welcome the important visitor from Zeviv Mountain.

As the two magistrates embraced each other with ceremonial cordiality, a retainer of the qadic took away the equine of the guest to a nearby stable. The personal guard of the Hegumen rode away to return to the Red Hat encampment a small distance outside of Rombucol.

The two officials went into the residence, where a table had been set with pastries, delicacies, and liqueurs. Only when the pair were seated did the Hegumen begin to reveal some of his plans to his host.

"I am here for one single purpose: to find and rescue my daughter and punish the miscreant who stole her from her home. So far, I have felt great disappointment with the inaction of the police in your city. They accomplish nothing, they report nothing at all. So, I have decided that I must take this business into my own hands of responsibility. There is no other way left."

The Hegumen took a long, large breath, then resumed.

"For that reason, I have decided to appropriate legal enforcement power in this city to myself. That is the only way to obtain the results I want and need."

The qadic gulped with astonishment. His face flushed red.

"Let me explain," continued the chief of the Red Hats. "All inspectors and patrollers shall be under my direct command during this investigation. My word will be law to all law enforcers in the city.

"All information connected with the search must be sent to me at once. No delay shall be allowed, none at all. I am supreme in this matter."

The qadic sat dumbfounded, staring in disbelief at the usurper of his power. How should he react to what was happening? It was best to keep a straight, stone face and make no comment whatsoever. He knew that he would get no sleep all that night.

"I plan to visit your police center tomorrow and question those in charge," announced Nomb Aacn. "Once I have sufficient information, I can make specific assignments and extend my investigation. I will keep in touch with you, as well."

"Thank you, sir," murmured the qadic with little energy, realizing the trouble ahead for Rocumbol.

Chapter V

Each day that passed, the company of amateur players rehearsed and tried out the drama on the stage of the Popular Theater.

The beginning section dealt with the escape of a novice visitor and the daughter of the Hegumen from an unnamed mountain claustrum.

Occasionally, there were interruptions by Frelo, the director, to make a suggestion to Yie and Joa as they acted out their roles. The amateur actors clung too close to their own memories of actual events, concluded the veteran dramatist. They had to think about how the future audience might misunderstand what they did or said in a staged surrounding. It could not be a simple reproduction of their lived history. The importance of timing and its effect in drama had to be taken into consideration, but not overemphasized. There had to be truth, but in heightened, dramatized form. Proper stylization was everything in staged enactment.

"Without loss of authenticity, you have to manage to make your movements, gestures, and vocal tone impressive and effective in the minds of those who will see you from out there in the auditorium," counseled the director, instructing them in the techniques of the acting craft.

Act Two presented new problems for the pair of lovers.

How were they to enact their relationship on the road to Caldaria Mountain? This was not supposed to be a play about romantic love. They must not even come close to that area, insisted Frelo. Nothing was to be allowed to divert the attention of the viewers from the focus upon the conflict with the Red Hats. The Hegumen chasing the pair of refugees was the primary villain, and a seasoned actor was to present him as a demonically evil force in the drama. Emotional romanticism was to be left to the creative imagination of each individual in the audience. It was not to be the focus of the play.

Practicing for the opening performance proved to be a difficult, exhausting labor. Patience on the part of all concerned was a necessity. The work was slow and demanding, not an easy thing to accomplish.

In the meantime, the danger of capture by Nomb Aacn grew.

The hunt for the fugitives became ever more concentrated and intense.

No one in the municipal police corps knew what to make of the Hegumen highlander who took effective control of them. Officers of rank had to take orders from an outsider, a stranger. Ordinary operations were turned upside down. The chain of command was made inoperative. Even the qadic himself was helpless against the human whirlwind from Zaviv Mountain.

Nomb, taking over an office in the central police station, made himself the central cog in the activities of all law enforcement personnel. His eyes read all written documents. He had drawings made and distributed of his daughter and her supposed abductor. A net of surveillance, entirely within his power, came into operation throughout the belower city.

Nomb increasingly ignored the qadic and all other city officials outside the police he had taken command of.

His final step was to bring in more Brothers from the Zeviv Claustrum. They were agents he could have complete trust in. These were personal friends who now exchanged their Red Hat garb for ordinary city costumes and clothing. They mingled among the belowers of Rocumbol, trying to melt into the crowds on the streets. These impersonators were easy to identify, despite all their efforts to appear as something they were not.

Caph spotted two of them on one of their excursions into the public eating places in the central sector of the city. He entered the restaurant named the Cuchara along with Cacique, the stage designer. The baaser was taking advantage of being in the city to try the cuisine of a variety of eateries. Cacique was desirous of reporting on the progress of his lighting project with the new plasmoid.

The pair took a booth recessed in the back wall of the place, adjacent to the noisy kitchen where busy cooks worked with breathtaking speed.

Cacique ordered roast of carnero for the two of them.

"The ram mutton is a rare dish of incredible taste," he told his companion. "No plate can compete with the carnero dishes of Rocumbol, believe me."

Once they were served and the waiter had walked away, Caph asked a question that his companion expected him to.

"Will the prismoids be ready by opening day?"

Cacique continued to eat as he answered this question.

"The work appears to be difficult and exacting. Many accidents and mistakes have already occurred. But I am assured by the glass-blower that all the separate pieces will be ready to put together in time."

"It will arrive close to when we need them, I imagine," said Caph between bites of mutton.

The stager gave an affirming nod.

It was at this point that the baaser saw two strange men step into the Cuchara and look around. The moment he spotted them, he saw through their unconvincing disguises. These had to be Red Hats from Zeviv posing as ordinary city-dwellers. But their true identity could not be hidden from him.

I must not stare at them, he told himself, because that would perhaps draw attention to myself, the last thing I want to happen.

It was a moment of supreme peril for him and his fellow escapees from Caldaria. What should he do? It was impossible to walk out, not having finished eating. He had to keep up a pretense of being someone not worthy of attention by the Red Hats.

Cacique sensed at once that there was something amiss.

"What is it my friend?" he gently asked, continuing to fill his mouth with food from his plate.

Caph answered in a low tone, without fear or alarm.

"I have reason to believe that the Red Hat pursuers of my group are combing Rocumbol for us. In fact, two secretives just came into the Cuchara. They have been seated far from us, over on the far side opposite our table. Do not look, it will only tend to draw attention this way. Believe me, the enemy is present right here in this restaurant."

"What are we going to do?" asked the other, desperation in his voice.

"Nothing. We must finish our dishes as if nothing has happened, as if we have not noticed they are here. Then, we pay our bill and saunter out as normally as we can.

"I think that you can shield me to a degree by walking on the inside, toward the center of this place while I take the outer position. Do not be afraid, we will manage it smoothly. Now, let's finish eating and make a quick exit out of here."

The next several minutes were tense and nervous ones.

When the waiter returned to ask if they wished to order anything else, both of them said that they did not. So, their bill was written and placed on the table. Caph took it and paid the man with spondulic coins from his purse.

Both customers rose simultaneously and made their way toward the entrance.

Cacique made a conscious effort to block anyone on the other side of the dining room from having a clear, direct view of his companion. Caph averted his face from that direction as much as was possible. They made it outside to the street without any incident.

One of the pair dared say something only when they had walked a distance away.

"What now?" whispered Cacique. "Did either of them see you in there?"

"I don't believe so, but how can I ever be certain?"

Another period of silence ensued, till they reached an intersection.

"I must go to the theater and warn our friends," softly muttered the baaser. "We will all have to take additional security measures from now on."

Cacique excused himself in order to make a visit to the workshop of Dijo.

Soon Caph arrived at the Popular Theater and entered through a back door. How was he going to relate his apprehensions to the others? he wondered. Would they accept a statement from him that he had crossed paths with badly disguised Red Hats?

Finding that a rehearsal of Act Three was in progress, he took a seat in the front row of the auditorium, a small distance from Director Frelo.

"Do not be afraid of displaying genuinely felt emotion," cried out the latter to the duo on stage. "But avoid overplaying, because a theater setting tends to magnify all moves and gestures. Take care not to overdo anything. That is a pitfall for even the best of actors. Be careful not to make that mistake."

The players continued until the end of the scene, when Frelo called out for a five-minute rest break. That was when Caph stood up and spoke.

"Excuse me for doing this, but I have something distressing to report."

All eyes centered on him as he described what he had seen a little while before. It was evident that Yie and Joa recognized the gravity of the danger he described to them. His words made a deep impression.

Frelo stood up. "No question but that greater care must be taken. We will have to move up the date of our opening by a week. That gives us less time to rehearse." He turned to the stage where Joa and Yie stood looking down into the pit. "Is that alright with the two of you?"

They both voiced their assent.

"We must work extra hours, with all our strength and energy," said Yie. "An increased effort has to be mounted by all of us."

"Let's go back to the next scene right now," said Frelo. "We have to hurry up and get the show ready in time."

Chapter VI

Dijo and his crew of workers transported the plasmoids, one by one, to the Popular Theater on horse-drawn wagons. Cacique accompanied the large transport wagon, then supervised the installation of the gigantic pieces of glass over the gas burners illuminating the stage.

Frelo, Caph, Yie, and Joa were present to watch and witness, burning with questions and curiosity. They waited impatiently to see the results of the glass-blowing project. Would the outcome be what they intended?

Cacique, once finished with the placement of all the plasmoids, stood on the front edge of the stage in order to give a short explanatory speech to all those present in the audience.

"I assign to these great, unusual prisms the function of polarizing and amplifying the corpuscles of light that will emanate from the gas flames once they begin burning. There will be a magnification and cleansing of the particles that originate in the combustion of the gas. It is a process that will line up the microscopic corpuscles in regulated, rectangular formations that then shine with renewed power and unprecedented clarity. The prismoids will divide the tiny bits of light, then recombine them into a new reticular pattern with a newly created shape and form.

"It is impossible for me to explain it fully, but the process can be demonstrated. That is exactly what I plan to do in the next several minutes."

Cacique climbed down off the stage and began to turn on each gas burner, lighting it with a vesta stick in his left hand. Whenever the match died out, he would light himself a new one. He held an entire box full of them in his hand.

The prismoids varied in size, from one foot to three in height.

As the gas burners were lighted and the house lanterns dimmed, light streamed forth over the stage, at different angles, in various directions, creating a startling, stunning brilliance.

Cacique continued standing at the middle of the stage in front of the footlights.

"Let me show you how versatile these prismoid pieces are," he told his small audience of comrades, watching with astonishment on their faces.

He proceeded to demonstrate the use of floats, wing lights, border lights, bunch lights, and focus beamers. Scenery prismoids could illustrate the backdrops in the rear of the stage. Focus lights provided a moveable spot that followed individual actors as they performed. All the different prismoids that Dijo had produced were placed in operation at once, till the stage became a crowded field of blinding light.

Then, Cacique shut off the gas supply of the lamps, one by one.

He looked out at his colleagues, a wide smile on his face.

"What do you people think of our new system?" he asked the stunned viewers. "Isn't it phenomenal? Tegumen has never before had such an ingenious method of stage lighting. It is something unprecedented. Everyone who sees these sights will be surprised and amazed. They shall have an experience they never had before."

Frelo suddenly rose to his feet and spoke.

"I want to start practicing with these prismoids. The cast has to become used to the intensity of illumination they will be working under. We will be using thus new method of lighting during the entire play and all its acts."

Yie and Joa rose and went toward the side steps leading to the stage.

There was a load of work ahead for them, both of the fugitives realized.

Caph, Yie, and Joa had become cautious and watchful when out in the open air. Public places accessible to everyone posed clear dangers to them. If Nomb Aacn was here in Rocumbol with a contingent of disguised agents, there was always a chance of being seen and identified. They had to be very careful.

The three fugitives went to the Public Theater long before the dawn of the short day, stayed there throughout the twilight hours, and only returned home to their apartments hours after the city lay in solid darkness. They dressed inconspicuously, as ordinary residents did. All their meals were prepared and eaten in private, along with other members of the cast.

The Hegumen grew ever more frustrated in his search for his daughter and those connected with her disappearance. He knew she had to be somewhere in the city. Why was it so difficult to locate her?

Nomb Aacn made frequent visits to the office suite of the qadic to complain of the slowness, clumsiness, and ineffectiveness of the Rocumbol police. He was not receiving the amount of cooperation that he needed and expected. That was the basis of numerous complaints to the local powerholder.

"What is it that you wish me to do?" asked the city official with exasperation. "I have ordered everything you requested to be carried out. Isn't that all that can be done?"

Nomb leaned forward in his chair. "I believe there is much more that is possible. For instance, money rewards can be offered to anyone providing useful tips that have investigative results. And there are special portions of your population who could be recruited for the hunt. For example, the children in the schools. We might organize them into squads to look for the refugees who are hidden in the city. Who knows where a useful clue might turn up? Anyone could be the key informant who spots these targets. We must use every person as a possible source of information."

No reply came immediately, for the qadic was meditating. How far was the highlander willing to go in his mania to get his daughter back? Was the outsider going to take over all power and authority in Rocumbol?

There was no finite limit to the man's thirst for cornering those he was after. Has Nomb Aacn gone mad? wondered the official forced by circumstances to cooperate with him.

"I will try the best I can to aid you, sir," promised the qadic with a great deal of inner reluctance and hesitation.

Yie rarely remembered any dream that occurred to him while asleep. But this one was clear and graphic. It dominated his mind when he awakened in the darkness of morning. The minute he saw Joa after going to her flat to share breakfast with her, the young man described and related it to her. There was a high level of excitement in his face, eyes, and voice.

"It was more a vision than a dream," he confessed to her. "It is connected directly to what we witnessed yesterday. I mean the stage lighting that Cacique demonstrated for us. My habit has always been to ignore dreams as fantasy and wishful-thinking. I do not take them seriously.

"My dream happened in Canara, where I was born and grew up. But my native dorp appeared transformed as I walked across it. The cottages were rebuilt and improved. Prosperity seemed general. Walls had fresh paint; what had previously been broken was now repaired.

"Even the sky appeared to have unusual brightness and color.

"Never before had I viewed this magnificent state when I lived there. What was the reason behind this phenomenon? That weighed upon me until the truth began to dawn on me. There was a new factor that did not exist before. A kind of illumination that did not exist before. A new sharpness was in my vision. I felt a great exhilaration in my heart. How was it being created? That was the question I asked myself.

"The answer came as an instant revelation. What did this new, lively light most resemble? It was a brightness coming from the prismoids brought into the Popular Theater by Cacique. The stage lighting we had witnessed there the day before was now shining radiantly in the world of my dream. The two conditions were identical. The new light in and over Canara was the result of something originating in prismoids.

"That was the conclusion I reached when I woke up. If only the dream had continued and I had witnessed more!"

All at once, Joa posed a question to him.

"What is the reality in what you saw, Yie? It was all a beautiful product of your imagination. What I think happened was that when you saw the new stage lighting, the image of it sank deeply into you. When you started to dream last night, it re-emerged in a fictional form. Your memory of Canara became the setting for a scene that you wished was true, even though it is impossible in actual life."

Yie frowned. "You think that was all it was, a phantom of the mind?"

"We must not take illusions for real things," she calmly said. "Our Tegumen is not a drama stage with scenery and footlights."

He was unable to make any reply.

Chapter VII

The final rehearsal before public performance was carried out with Cacique providing prismatic stage lighting. Everyone present realized how serious their last run-through was.

Act Four rolled toward its end with Yie and Joa at the front of the stage. The pair looked off-stage, toward what they imagined to be the city of Rocumbol.

"There it lies, our destination," said Yie with an explosion of emotions. "Caph promised us we will be safe once we are there. But is that going to happen? How can our future be foretold? What if we are followed and captured once inside the city?"

Yie took her hand in his.

"There is nothing for us to dread, Joa. It cannot be more dangerous there than where we have already been. The days ahead of us cannot be full of greater peril than those that are now past and gone. We have to buckle up our courage and march on. There is no other alternative. We have to fight for our future."

She gazed into his face pleadingly.

"Together, we go on to whatever awaits us," Joa softly muttered.

"That's the spirit that will take us forward."

Hand in hand, the two refugees walked off to the right until they were out of sight. The prismatic spotlight manned by Cacique followed them to the end of the stage.

In the first row of the audience, Frelo stood up.

"Excellent!" he called out loudly. "We are ready for tomorrow night. Now, let's all go and get a good night's sleep."

In a short time, when the practice had ended, the cast and crew left the theater.

Yie, Joa, and Caph departed into the thickening darkness as a group of three, making for the building that contained their rented flats.

They trudged along in silence. But suddenly Caph made a surprising proposal to the other two.

"It would be great to have ourselves a little celebration now that all the rehearsals are finished. I think we should stop at a bistro or pub and have some drinks to tide us over till tomorrow evening. We have certainly earned a bit of relaxation."

Surprisingly, Joa seconded the idea and made the choice of where to go. "That's just what we need at this moment. And there's a sign that points to where we should go. Look, the name of that place is the Pharos, the lantern. I consider that a good omen," she said with a laugh, "because tomorrow we will be working under a beacon coming from the prismoids of Cacique. So, let's go in there and refresh ourselves."

Yie, doubtful of the wisdom of the proposal, did not object to what his companions had accepted without asking him. Thus he was swept up into the Pharos by the other two. They were taking a heedless risk, he realized but failed to tell them.

Music from a hurdy-gurdy filled the smoky air of the small pub. A crowd of drinkers took up the chairs and stools of the front area. The three who entered only found empty space in the back, at a corner table. The smoke from bhang, boxthorn, stramony, and cubeb cigarettes filled the air, making it hard to see very far.

Soon after they sat down, a waiter in a yellow apron came up and asked the group for their orders.

"A tall glass of cervezix beer for me," said Caph with a grin. He looked at Joa, then at Yie.

"I'll have the same," said first the former, then the latter.

When the waiter had left, Joa began to speak in a lowered tone.

"It is no secret that I would have liked a different ending to the play. The impression may be created that all difficulties and dangers are past, that they have overcome and conquered their troubles with the highland oppressors. How can we honestly say that when we know it is not true?"

Yie bit his lip. "You are thinking of the Red Hats who still are here in Rocumbol? Who continue to search and hunt for us?"

"That shadow has not yet passed, has it?" she murmured softly.

Caph now intervened. "Let's not think of such things at this time. The two of you have great responsibilities tomorrow at the theater. After that, we can deal with the danger from the highlanders. We will then be better prepared to deal with our foes from the mountains."

The waiter appeared with a tray of drinks for them, so the trio stopped their conversation.

But enough had already been said to draw the concentrated interest of two patrons of the Pharos sitting at a short distance away, but whose presence was concealed from the fugitives by a large potted plant positioned between the two groups and tables.

The unseen listeners set to memory all they picked up through their ears. Both were later able to report every word and sentence of their three neighbors. They paid complete attention to the task, for the pair were disguised undercover espials on the payroll of the city police. They were informers experienced in picking up useful information.

Once Caph, Yie, and Joa were finished drinking, they left for their flats. Their mood was lighter as they looked ahead to the morrow. They shared a growing optimism about what would happen.

As soon as they were gone, the two behind the aspidistra also rose. They knew that they had overheard something of importance that their superiors in the administrative hierarchy would be pleased to know about.

The Red Hats had assigned a plainclothes Brother to the central police station to keep an eye on all overnight communications and reports coming in or going out. It was that individual who was present in the command room when the two espials reported to the night officer on what they had picked up in the Pharos.

"These people are engaged in play-acting on the stage?" asked the astounded commander of police. His almond eyes expanded as if exploding.

"It sounded to me as if they were talking about the Popular Theater. At least that was the clear implication of what we heard them saying."

"And they were at rehearsals before stopping for drinks?"

"The final, last rehearsals for a play beginning tomorrow, after dark."

The police official looked the one, then the other, in the face and studied the expressions they presented to him.

"These three people match the descriptions given us by the Red Hats?"

"As far as we could see," answered the espial. "We could not afford to look at them directly without setting off their sense of alarm. We had to take extra care not to be detected by them."

The officer in charge thought a moment. "I have to report this to the qadic himself. He will want to know, then decide what to do about it."

Another person who was present already knew what he had to accomplish.

The Red Hat in civilian clothes slipped out of the station, heading for the encampment of the Brothers on the outskirts of Rocumbol.

Nomb Aacn was not yet asleep in his tent, so that he did not have to be awakened in order to receive the important, urgent message.

When the qadic awoke a little after the next dawning, he was surprised when his wife informed him that the Red Hat Hegumen was downstairs, waiting to see him about police business.

He put on a bedrobe and hurried down the stairs to where Nomb sat awaiting him. The highlander's face was the color of a ripe beet. This was an indicator of some kind of crisis.

"They are located and about to be caught in our nets," said the Hegumen, rising out of the quercine chair that he rested in. "It appears that the fugitives are involved in putting on a play at a city theater. They were overheard referring to an opening performance this evening. I have sent agents to learn exactly when that will be. By that time, our trap will be set. I have ordered the Brothers to surround the theater, both mounted and on foot. There will be no way of escape. Every precaution shall be taken to ensure that nothing goes wrong. All of them will be captured."

Nomb looked at the qadic with iron determination. "We will need re-enforcements from the city police. They cannot be in uniform. We will close in on the targets with a solid noose. Do you see what I mean?"

"Yes," meekly said the city magistrate.

Why had he not been awakened and told of this? the qadic wondered. Have the Red Hats taken over the complete administration of the law? Have they taken over my beloved city?

It was then that a noisy knocking at the front door occurred. A servant opened it and let in three policemen who were there to inform the qadic of the report that had been sitting at the station for many hours. As he listened to the belated message, the dumbfounded qadic pondered where his duty and loyalty truly lay.

Chapter VIII

Excitement gripped everyone involved with the first enactment of the play called "Caldaria". No author's name was given on the printed notices that announced the premiere. There was no need to say that it was the joint creation of a group whose members were going to represent themselves on the stage of the Popular Theater. The audience had a good idea what they were going to be witnesses to. This was not going to be the usual, customary theatrical presentation of some familiar classic.

Caph, Yie, and Joa arrived hours before the curtain was to go up.

In separate rooms in the rear corridor, the cast prepared themselves for the coming performance. Not much in the way of makeup would be needed. The primary costumes were to be what the fugitives had brought along with them. In a short while, both Yie and Joa were ready. The former entered the room of his partner to talk with her, hoping to raise her confidence. Encouragement was his goal.

"I wanted to see you alone before we go on," he explained. "How are you holding up, dear Joa?"

She turned about completely and faced him.

"I'm excited, as you probably also are. But once the play starts, I am sure that all nerves will be calmed. How are you doing, Yie?"

"My thoughts dwell on something else. Can you guess what it is? I'll tell you, Joa. My dream, the one I described to you yesterday."

"Did you have the same dream again?" she anxiously asked.

"No, that isn't it. But I've pondered and pondered. What it might have been was a kind of preview of where our planet is headed. Of the future that is destined to come about on Tegumen for all its inhabitants."

"What do you mean by that?" she inquired in a puzzled tone.

"Our life shared here below might become one of bright light that lasts many hours, if only we could apply prismoids the way that Cacique does. Am I only fantasizing about what is impossible and can never be? Has my imagination begun to run wild and lose itself in fantastic dreams? I wonder."

She stared at him in silence, unable to give an answer.

"I don't know," she finally whispered. "There is no way for anyone to predict until a try is made. What do you think? It appears to me that these prismoids are replacing the idea of the silver-platinum plates in your thinking."

"We have not lost possession of all the plates we once had," said Yie with an audible moan. "And there is a chance we may be able in coming days to try to use them again. Who can tell?."

Before she could reply, a voice in the corridor made the first curtain call.

Yie and Joa stepped out of the dressing room and headed for the stage.

When Nomb Aacn appeared on the back of an equine only twenty span from the entrance to the Popular Theater, he was surprised to see a cordon of uniformed municipal police guarding the doorways. He turned to his mounted companion Red Hat for an explanation.

"These patrollers appeared here only a few minutes ago and took command of all entrances and exits on all four sides of the building. When they were asked their purpose, the officer in charge told us that they are here to assist us in the mission we were sent on. So that no one can slip out unseen and undetected, all these men are about to guard and watch. What do you think we should be doing, sir?"

Nomb considered a moment, then answered him.

"Whether we are joining with them or they are joining with us, it will be all the same. The noose around those we are after is now solid and complete. We must be ready for whatever occurs when the time comes to capture them."

The Hegumen lowered himself down from his equine and walked over to where the unmounted Brothers stood in a group, a short distance from the policemen besieging the Popular Theater.

Yie and Joa stood together at stage center, behind the unraised curtain. It was only seconds until action was to begin. Both primary personae were breathing hard. Anticipation was more difficult than what might come later.

He held her right hand tightly in his own, attempting to lift her courage and spirit, as well as his own.

A slight noise indicated to them that ropes were moving. The curtain began to move to the side. Brilliant prismoidal light shone into the eyes of both actors. Yie and Joa looked beyond the edge of the stage to the audience sunken in darkness. They seemed to be hunting for some sign or signal from somewhere.

Neither actor noticed that an unidentified figure came on stage from the left side. It was a small man in a formal cutaway, a bright yellow sash around the waist of his dark serge coat.

He looked out beyond the prismoids and spoke in a loud, sonorous voice.

"Citizens of Rocumbol present here in the Popular Theater for the performance of a new drama, I am your qadic with a sad, tragic announcement to make before you.

"I have come to officiate at a juridical arrest that shall presently be carried out by our faithful police. Let me explain.

"The pair of actors behind me are not members of our community. Nor are they professional thespians with experience on stage. No, they are something quite different.

"They have come to Rocumbol in flight from the lawful authorities of Zeviv Mountain. Many Brothers of that claustrum are outside this theater, waiting for the apprehension of these two.

"They have traveled a long distance for the arrest of these people. Duty to my office and the laws of the city oblige me to take immediate action. So, I hereby arrest the two actors you see before you. The police guards with me shall take custody of them at the present time. They shall be placed under arrest and taken to our city prison for immediate interrogation and investigation.

"I am sorry to inform you that there shall be no play on stage tonight. You can go home in peace. There are patrollers outside the theater and on all the primary avenues. I advise all of you to leave and disperse. The official police officers of our community shall enforce and maintain public peace and order this evening and through the night. Thank you for your cooperation."

No one seemed prepared to move immediately.

Yie and Joa stood gaping in astonishment as a squad of policemen surrounded them. "Come with us, please," said their captain in official yellow uniform.

"Where are you taking us?" demanded Yie in an angry voice.

The qadic had by now turned around and moved closer.

"First of all, to my own residence," he told the surprised pair under arrest.

The audience fled from the theater in disorder, rushing through adjoining streets and preventing the Red Hats from moving forward to make arrests on their own. An undefined fear created general panic. Nomb Aacn and his cohorts found themselves unable to advance into the Popular Theater. They had no idea what had caused this evacuation or what was happening inside the building. The frantic exiting was an unexpected surprise to them.

Director Frelo managed to lead Caph and Cacique to his office in the rear, hoping that there would be safety for them there. But where were Yie and Joa, the objectives of the Red Hats? What had happened to them?

A squad of a dozen police patrollers had stepped out onto the stage, surrounding them. Under previously issued orders, the prisoners were escorted through the rear door of the theater, down an alley, into a back street that had been closed to pedestrians and traffic.

After a few minutes, the pair were marched into the residence of the qadic, the man who could determine their fate.

The wife of the magistrate had a repast prepared for the disoriented Joa and Yie. She led them into the large dining room where the arrestees were served. Both were so nervous they could hardly eat.

"Do not be concerned, my husband has taken on the responsibility for your well-being," she told her house guests, smiling at them with feelings of hospitality. "He does not intend to surrender the self-rule of Rocumbol to these terrible highlanders. We rule ourselves here. That has always been our way."

Joa looked up from the table and asked the woman a question.

"What is going to happen to us?"

"The problem is to find a secure and secret haven where these mountain tormentors cannot follow or take hold of you. The qadic is searching for such a place. One where you two can be well hidden, that no one will suspect is your refuge."

"We are safe here in your mansion?" asked Yie.

"For the time being, at least," muttered the wife of the qadic.

The loud noise of a door opening signaled the entrance into the house of the top municipal official.

"He has returned," said the wife. "You will soon learn what his plans are for your transport elsewhere."

Both Yie and Joa stopped eating and looked into each other's faces.

What will happen to us now? Where will we be sent?

As the qadic, the yellow sash of office about his waist, rushed into the dining room, the rescued pair held their breaths. They waited to hear what their future was to be. What was he going to say to the two fugitives?

Chapter IX

Tegumen, a planet lacking seas and oceans, depended upon a multitude of lakes to hold its reserves of water. These were scattered across the sphere, but there were regions of particularly large bodies of water. In the far northern latitudes, the Doigt Lakes were large and concentrated near each other. They gave this region its name and character.

Yie and Joa learned that night that the qadic of Rocumbol was arranging their transportation by freight wagon to the shores of Lake Digit, at the center of the lake system. To the south of it lay Lake Index, Medus, Ponce, Orteil, Annular, and Auricular.

"The six lakes that intervene should discourage the Red Hats from searching for you there," the magistrate assured them. "Geography will serve you as protector. There should be no intrusions by them thereabout. That is my hope: that all of you will be safe there."

A little before the late dawn, a cartage wagon came to the back door of the official residence to pick up the two passengers for the north.

Yie arranged it so that their extra clothes and the three silver platinum plates were taken from their rented room and brought to be transported with them on the vehicle.

"There will be room for you at a lakeside hotel with which I have had dealings," explained the qadic. "I and my wife wish you good fortune there. Your safety should be assured. The place is the most secure location I can think of. Geography should furnish an excellent form of protection there."

The wagon, traveling over short day and long night, was soon in areas that neither fugitive had ever been in before. The forests that surrounded the dirt road were coniferous varieties of firs, junipers, piceans, blue sapins, and abeths. Their natural beauty was peaceful and inspiring. The population here was small and scattered about.

The two drivers who took turns at the reins of the equines furnished food for their passengers. Occasional stops allowed Joa and Yie to see how the mountains and forests were changing as they traveled north. The peaks became lower. Many had no claustrum settlements on top. Vegetation was quite different. Cone trees came to predominate on all sides.

Yie, holding Joa tightly, attempted to reassure her.

"We cannot go back, so we have to place our hopes on this new place. That is the way things are. The life of many a person, over the ages, has necessitated adjustment to new conditions in unfamiliar places. Think of how our ancestors had to settle on a new planet totally strange to them. That was a daring adventure that they lived through back then. We are in a different era completely."

"What will we do at Lake Digit, Yie?" she asked with trepidation.

"That remains to be seen," he smiled, "but it will be up to us. That is the way it always is, everywhere."

She gave a nod, snuggling into his embrace.

LIGHT UP THE VALLEYS

The hotel on the lake shore consisted of a series of separate cottages. Around it, on three sides, rose steep mountains of middle height covered with tall pines. The panorama was a magnificent one.

The senior driver of their wagon told them to wait while he entered the main building and gave the owner a letter from the qadic of Rocumbol.

Yie helped Joa climb out of the rear of the vehicle. They absorbed the purity and clarity of the northern landscape. It was the short daytime and the skies contained more light than they were used to. This was a result of the lower height of the mountains hereabout. Yet the night ahead was long and the day only minutes in duration, as elsewhere on the planet.

"I have never seen a twilight as bright as that," commented Joa. "But don't you feel a sharp chill in the air?"

"Yes. It's a paradox. This latitude has a quarter hour more of day, but the average temperature is lower than further south."

They looked out over Lake Digit. Both noticed the shimmering glare far out on the water. The heliac shone down in a manner unfamiliar to them. There was an eerie tone about it.

The noise of an opening door attracted their attention. They watched as the driver approached, a lanky skeleton of a man in black business suit next to him.

"Welcome to our lake and hotel," said the stranger, his voice high and rough. "I am fortunate to have a vacant cottage available that can be shared by the two of you. Let me first introduce myself, though.

"I am Gui, owner and manager of the hotel you see. You have had a view of the lake already. Isn't it splendid? There is grandeur in all directions. The scenery here is priceless.

"As you know, the qadic of Rocumbol wrote introducing you and asking that I provide the best accommodations I can. That I shall do. I consider him one of my dearest friends. And now I shall include the two of you in my ring of friends. Welcome to Lake Digit. Now, let's go into the hotel grill and feed you some northern cuisine. Please follow me."

Yie and Joa said farewell to the two drivers and entered the building with its owner, Gui. Both of them already felt much better. They had reached a safe haven, they believed.

Cervine steak with raw rugals provided a most satisfying meal. Gui gave them a description of what they could expect in this latitude new to them.

"Although our day is a little longer than further south, the night is as dark here as anywhere on Tegumen. Perhaps we can see more in twilight, but that is all. There is no escape from the night when it comes."

"We saw for ourselves a great shining light in the waters of your lake," interjected Joa. "Is that a sight that disappears along with the heliac?"

Gui turned and gave her a curious look. "That mirror effect on the water is at the center of Lake Digit, where the shadows of the mountains do not reach. That is a place where daylight shines for at least twelve full hours, as it would everywhere if the mountains did not exist. Only out there in the middle of the lake waters are day and night of equal length. This hotel and the shore are, unfortunately, overshadowed by the peaks and fall into full darkness."

Joa posed another question. "Does your region contain Red Hat claustra as in the south?"

"Only about half of our summits do. The other half do not." Gui, all at once, thought of something. "Would you like to take a boat excursion out in the water? If you are tired, it can wait until you two are fully rested. I own a sail sloop that I can take you out on. What do you say?"

Both Joa and Yie replied they were ready to go out with him the very next day. Neither of them needed any extended rest. They were both invigorated by this environment new to them. What might it hold of value for their future? both of them wondered.

Caph, aware of the personal danger should the Red Hats get hold of him, tried to stay out of public places where they might cross his path. But he judged it safe to go shopping at the central farmers' market for food. Being in a crowd gave him adequate protection, he told himself. He was one person among so many others.

He changed his mind once on the scene.

Hawkers called out offered prices, praising their wares as the best anywhere. Customers haggled with sellers. Unending hubbub filled the air of the square during the short hour of twilight. Bodies hurried in all directions in the short interval of trade.

It was too late when Caph realized the presence of mounted Red Hats.

From all sides, the market square was surrounded. In seconds, there began a fine, careful search of all faces. The crowd was trapped in the market.

Caph made a serious error when he tried to slip away unnoticed.

The youngest of the Brothers, an inexperienced novice, was first to catch sight of him. "There goes the baaser!" he shouted to his comrades.

Several riders sent their equines toward the fleeing figure, easily cornering him against the wall of a downtown store.

Caph realized he was caught and had no hope of escape. But before he could be taken, the novice rider barreled into him as if his equine was no longer under control.

The catastrophe that happened could not have been foreseen. The heavy weight of an equine falling on him crushed the life out of the victim in less than a second.

"You idiot!" yelled the Red Hat captain. "You've killed a fugitive we had right in our hands. What do we do now?"

Gui let his sloop drift lazily in the middle of Lake Digit. From overhead came strong, bright rays, unlike any that Yie or Joa had ever seen before.

"How marvelous it is out here!" said Joa. "If only all of Tegumen could enjoy this light. It is the unshadowed heliac that all the belowers of the planet deserve to see."

"But they don't," noted Yie. "Only in dreams like the one I told you of is that true. That is the tragedy we live with."

"It has always been so, since our ancestors migrated," said Gui thoughtfully. "Perhaps they chose the wrong planet for their home."

Yie grimaced. "It was the Red Hats who made that decision. Our people had no voice in it. And so, we are condemned to twilight and darkness, unless…"

"Your dream comes true?" said Joa excitedly. "Can prismoids liberate us?"

Yie did not give her an answer because he was engaged in deep consideration of new projects and ideas whose value he did not yet know.

Chapter X

Frelo stayed in his apartment without going outside in the days after the closing down of the Popular Theater. He believed that safety from the Red Hat invaders was guaranteed him there in his digs. Why would they ever hunt for him? He had done nothing specific against the highlanders. They were after the couple who were fugitives from Zeviv Mountain. That was the prize they were after, not someone like himself.

But he might be identified as an ally of the fugitives. So, it was wise for him to lie low till he knew for sure what the situation was. That appeared safest and wisest to him.

Frelo nearly panicked when a loud, heavy knock sounded at his door.

Two uniformed city patrollers stood there.

"You are Frelo, Director at the Popular Theater?"

"Yes," gulped the overwhelmed resident of the apartment.

"Do not be alarmed, you are not under arrest or in police custody. We are here under orders from the city qadic himself. He wishes to see you as soon as possible, at your convenience, and we are to escort you to a place where the two of you can talk in private. Are you prepared to go with us right now?"

Frelo gave a nod, then asked to get his overcoat and flat skimmer hat. Soon the three men were on their way. Their specific destination was a mystery to the drama director. Why did the qadic wish to see him? he wondered.

An obscure bookshop on a side alley was the secret meeting spot set for this clandestine purpose.

His escorts took Frelo to a back storage room where the magistrate sat waiting.

The two men shook hands and the qadic asked his guest to sit down. By then the two police patrollers were outside, guarding the store from intruders.

"We had to meet this way in order to protect you," said the qadic. "Already, the Red Hats have killed the baaser from Caldaria Mountain called Caph. I want no more bloodshed in this city. That is why I wish to offer you safe passage elsewhere."

"Where can I go?" said Frelo. "Who will hide me? Won't the Red Hats chase after me in time?"

"I have already sent Yie and Joa to a secure haven. It is up in the northern lake region. Would you wish to join them there?"

"They could not track any of us to that area?" asked the director.

"I doubt they would or could," said the official reassuringly.

"There is only one thing, though."

"What is that?"

"I brought my stage designer, Cacique, into this trouble. Could he go with me? I have a moral obligation to provide him protection and shelter."

"Certainly," said the qadic. "He shall go to Digit Lake along with you. Both of you fellows will be safe and protected there."

Frelo was soon escorted by the patrollers to the wagon service that was to take him on his long journey to the lake district. He waited at the vehicle for the designer to join him.

Soon the two theater professionals were repeating the trip taken earlier by Joa and Yie.

Nomb Aacn summoned his superior officers to the Red Hat encampment outside Rocumbol and made an announcement that shook all of them.

"The unfortunate death of one of the criminals has created an unprecedented situation in the city. I have decided we must act at once to establish order there. So, as of dusk today I am assuming government power over all of Rocumbol. I am ordering that the qadic be put in retirement and all his authority be transferred over to me. This is done under my office of Hegumen of Zeviv Mountain and its claustrum. We all know that the valleys of Tegumen are not legally independent, but are mere parts and extensions of our conventicle communities up above. They are our dependents and subordinates.

"I therefore assume the office of acting qadic and governor of this troubled city. My purpose is to apprehend those we came here to capture. I can only fulfill my task of recovering my daughter by completely searching the city. That will only occur if our Red Hats appropriate total police power over the population. The ordinary official hierarchy of Rocumbol is hereby put in suspension and is not to act or decide anything.

"Tomorrow we start a house-to-house, building-to-building search."

Astonishment remained high among the Red Hats for a considerable time. It was now their job to carry out this order for a take-over of power. No one could predict what the results and implications might turn out to be.

Joa was still asleep when Yie went out to the beach to watch the rise of the heliac. He had never seen a similar imposing display of natural light. Red, orange, amethyst, gold, saffron, mauve, magenta, and many other hues were sighted by him. It was an unprecedented experience for Yie.

But a sudden, unexpected pain struck him at the center of his head.

Most of the people of Tegumen who lived in the valleys would never see such a rising of the heliac for themselves. The warm energy of real day was absent from their lives, from birth till the ending at death. They dwelled mainly in darkness and shadow. For them, the heliac star was a fleeting, short experience in a life ruled by twilight and night.

Belowers existed under the limits of restricted light and energy.

A distant voice seemed to be telling Yie that he had a special mission. It was an impossibly difficult task, one that perhaps he could never finish.

Should he start on it, even though the odds were against any success?

For he would face the solid, united opposition of every claustrum on the summits. The conflict would be terribly harsh and merciless. Years of painful hardship loomed ahead for the fugitive if he took up the plan forming in his mind.

This challenge had to be taken up. There was no alternative for him.

Joa was already his first convert to the cause he had conceived, that of radically altering the foundation of life on Tegumen.

The qadic of Rocumbol was dumbfounded by what his assistant told him.

"The Red Hats are pasting up proclamations on all the message boards," he trembled. "They are announcing the transfer of supreme power to their Hegumen."

Rising from his chair, the qadic was about to walk around his quercine desk when the door to his office flew open. Five men quickly marched in, the last of whom was Nomb Aacn himself. The latter blocked the way forward for the qadic. He began shouting in an extremely loud voice.

"As Hegumen of Zeviv, I pronounce this city part of my domain and assume the office of municipal chief. No longer are you to act in any official manner. Your post is vacated, all of its jurisdiction and authority fall to me alone. Any resistance to this order will be instantly suppressed and crushed. Is my meaning clear to you?"

Unable to say anything, the city magistrate retreated several steps.

By then, two large Red Hats had advanced far enough to take hold of him on both sides. There was no need to tell the qadic that he was under arrest.

How could he not know it?

Frelo and Cacique conversed as the wagon they were on neared the region of northern lakes and its cool atmosphere.

"What shall we do to sustain ourselves once we reach our destination?" asked Frelo. "I know nothing beyond work on the theater stage, that is all that I have ever worked at."

"There are no theaters this far north?"

"It is a very poor latitude. The population cannot afford high culture and the advanced arts. There will be little economic opportunity for us here."

Cacique ruminated a moment.

"Why don't I set up a light show of some sort? That would surely draw some sort of audience, I am certain."

"We will have to take it up with Yie and Joa," said Frelo. "They will have suggestions of their own. They were very interested in prismoids, weren't they?"

Cacique nodded yes, remembering his conversations with them at the Popular Theater. "We will be seeing our friends shortly, Frelo," he told his traveling companion.

Part 4

Chapter I

Gui entered the shore veranda where his two guests were sitting, looking out at the shimmering, sparkling surface of Lake Digit.

"I have a surprise for both of you," he announced. "A wagon just arrived here from Rocumbol. The driver has a letter from the qadic introducing two additional escapees from the Red Hats. Both of them are acquaintances of yours. At the moment, they are having a hearty repast in the dining room. I promised to find and fetch you two. So, follow me and see who they are."

Joa and Yie sprang up with excitement in their eyes, curious to find out who had just arrived. When they saw for themselves, both reddened with instant joy. Yie spoke first.

"Frelo! Cacique! It can't be true. How did you get here? Was it difficult to escape the Red Hats who took over in Rocumbol?"

"We came the same way that you did, by wagon from the city," answered Cacique with a self-satisfied grin.

"We were in danger but the qadic rescued us," explained Frelo. "The bad news is the assassination of Caph. The Red Hats showed him no mercy at all."

"He was killed?" said Joa with shock on her face.

"Run down like a dog by equines," explained Cacique. "My friend and I are dedicated to avenging his slaughter. We are in perpetual war with those inhuman monsters. They are doing horrible, unforgettable things."

"We are at war, likewise," declared Yie.

All four of them thought for a moment. Finally, Yie spoke again.

"I want both of you to experience an extraordinary phenomenon. Light from the heliac that lasts for an unusual length of time. When you have witnessed it, you will agree with me about how this light can be our weapon of final victory over the Red Hats. It will be a hard, onerous effort I have in mind, but we can and must carry it through. That is the sole hope left us and all the belowers on this planet."

Puzzled over his meaning, the newly arrived men finished eating, then went out to the veranda with their friends to observe the rapidly waning light of day.

"Tomorrow," began Yie, "our hotelier will take you out on the waters to see the glowing reflection of the heliac at its brightest. It will be an astounding sight that will inspire and enchant you. There is nothing like it anywhere.

After breakfast, at dawn, Gui took Frelo and Cacique onto his sail sloop. Yie and Joa went onto the veranda and sat on long chairs, watching the boat move slowly toward the middle of the lake. As the heliac rose into the whitish sky, the watery surface shone ever more brighter, ever more gleaming. It was then that Joa suddenly asked a question.

"Even if they become convinced to join with us, where will we find the resources needed for such a grand project? You have no mazuma, and neither do I. How can we pay for all that will be necessary?"

Yie turned his head and smiled at her.

"I haven't been thinking too practically, but there are ways to do that. For instance, we can ask for voluntary contributions, starting right here around Lake Digit. Then, we might turn to the population of the entire region of these lakes. Our reach can expand wider and wider. There will be no limit to it.

"I know that this is a region of severe poverty. But the people around the lake will be the earliest beneficiaries of our effort. Our request can be in the form of loans that someday will be repaid. We will have to convince the donors of the feasibility of our plan. That may take a lot of work for us to accomplish. The enterprise will not be an easy one at all.

"Perhaps it will be possible to convert the belowers of the northern zone to a new type of faith."

"A new type of faith?" returned Joa. "What do you mean?"

"We have to instill in belowers the idea that the light of the heliac is for all of Tegumen, not just for the peaks and the summits above. That the mountains are not an inevitable barrier fated to be eternal obstacles for us.

"If we succeed in inspiring the common villagers with hope in the coming abundance of light, there will result a flood of contributions. That will produce the financial support to build the system that we dream of."

"You believe all of that possible, Yie?"

"We must trust and believe that it will happen. Our promise to the belowers will not be merely a material one, but will also bring spiritual enlightenment. Everyone can share in the higher reality and infinite joy we will provide. No one shall be left out."

"The prospective is breathtaking," said Joa. "We will be able to bring about a new vital energy and illumination of minds. There shall be both material and nonmaterial progress for our people. It will be like starting all over again."

"We will start working right away," said Yie with confidence in his voice.

The sailing sloop now began to move back to the hotel shore.

When Cacique and Frelo returned, they were full of energetic enthusiasm.

"I know how to get the prismoids that will be needed," said Cacique over the dinner table. All four refugees sat with the proprietor, Gui. The group had advanced to specific plans on how to move forward.

"Dijo, the glassmaker, must be convinced to make us the components for a large screen of prismoids," continued the stage designer. "If necessary, I am willing to go back to Rocumbol and get him to work with us. He is a courageous man and will dare to join and cooperate. He is the type who will donate his own labor and materials, I know that. He has that kind of personal strength of character."

"Let us start first with written messages," suggested Yie. "There is no need to expose anyone in the city to unnecessary risk."

Joa then asked a question. "A screen will be built to catch the heliac light, but how will it be moored on the lake?"

"The waters out there are calm and quiet," said Gui. "I believe that a flat barge will be adequate to support even a large screen at a stable level."

"We can eventually have several barges with multiple screens," mused Yie aloud. "Perhaps the final form can be a wall of many screens across the center of Lake Digit. It could be built on buoys and floats. I can envision a pontoon bridge under a series of prismoidal screens, reaching to a considerable height and extending the width of the lake. It will be a magnificent structure."

"But all of that remains in the sphere of speculation until we reach that point. For the time being, we must concentrate on the production of basic glass prismoids. That is the first important stage.

"And the new, enhanced heliac light may turn out to make practical application of the silver platinum plates. That could be the key to making them practical for our planet."

It appeared that everyone there agreed on what was to be done.

Fear and shock reigned over Rocumbol. Even the traditional city police force was terrorized by the all-powerful Red Hats. All sense of confidence and security disappeared with the coming of the highlanders with their oppressive direct rule.

Taking over the official residence from the now imprisoned qadic, Nomb Aacn had little time for sleeping in the magistrate's ornate bedroom. He was awake and busy for long hours, leading and taking part in the search for the supposed abductors in control of his daughter. The more the hunt was frustrated, the greater his feverish efforts to uncover where she might be hidden within the city.

The idea that she was gone from there never took form in his mind.

Nomb drew the strings of power ever tighter in his own hands.

Not only the Popular, but all public theaters were indefinitely closed.

The police patrollers operated with one lone assignment: to locate the trail of Joa and those who had her in captivity, and to take back control of her.

Stores, houses, libraries, offices, and warehouses were broken into, even when locked up or closed. No building was exempt from intrusion. The pace of the hunting rose at a spiraling speed. A frenzy characterized it. The aim of finding the fugitives came to have absolute, final priority.

Yet no success at all came to the anxious Red Hats and their exhausted, haggard Hegumen. He could not have stopped what he had begun, even if he so desired. The madness had an inertia all its own and continued on and on. There appeared to be no relief or escape of any kind for the belower city.

Chapter II

Dijo received the letter from Cacique through the wagon drivers. He sent back word that he would be happy to construct the prismoids desired and have them transported to Lake Digit.

"He is adamant in his opposition to the new tyranny in Rocumbol. This new project will be his way of fighting back against it," commented the wagoner upon returning with the glassmaker's answer.

That was heartening news for the originating group in the far north. Their next goal was to win the support of the local population, who would provide aid and protection to them.

It was decided that Yie was to attend a series of meetings in different dorps to address the belowers who lived there.

The first was held in the small hamlet of Petai, only a few furlongs from the lake. Yie arrived after the fall of the heliac. He spoke to a small group gathered in a hut on the periphery of the settlement. They listened to his words with rapt attention.

"My dear fellow-believers, we are descendants of some of the same type of ancestors as you are, those brought to Tegumen long ago by the Red Hats. They were to be the laborers and cultivators, settled in the valleys where crops and sheep could be raised. But the leaders of the migration did not foresee what the conditions were to be below the mountains. As a result of their ignorance, our predecessors did not know that they would be exploited, repressed, and frustrated. The dorps that our people built became their jails, their prisons. Today, we are the same as prisoners. Our lives go on in the darkness of night, with only a brief moment of twilight each day. We are people lost in a world of darkness.

"But is that our inevitable fate? There is one way out that has leaped before our eyes only recently. What if the period of light could be made both brighter and longer? What if the darkness were limited to only half of the daily cycle of time? What if new rays of hope appeared for us?

"Our work would then become different. New opportunities would open up for creative production. Heliac energy would be available and we could attempt to catch and apply it. A greater, more varied system of life would appear. There would be a scale of activity never experienced here before. All belowers could feel unprecedented optimism. Higher happiness and fulfillment. All these would belong to the majority of Tegumen dwellers."

Yie paused a few seconds, then went on. The dorfers, waiting with expectancy, silently listened to hear more.

"Yes, my brothers and sisters, there is a way to bring the heliacal corpuscular to your valley. You know of the comparatively immense illumination above Lake Digit. My colleagues and I have a plan by which we can bring that same light to you on a horizontal level. This can have revolutionary results in the lives we live if it is harnessed and tamed.

"Think how it can change everything. A new energy would arrive to activate all of you. New possibilities and options, new industries and products will become practical realities. Life would take on a new coloring for all of us. It will not have the character displayed these many centuries down to today.

"Let us join together, let us unite so all our efforts can be combined. The future of the planet depends upon you. Unless we take action, things will continue the way they have for eons of time. Do not let that happen.

"I call upon all who hear my voice to become soldiers in an army of light, working and fighting for victory over darkness. It will be a battle for the shape of the future, nothing less than that."

The listeners remained motionlessly still for a short while. Then, one villager rose to step forward to congratulate Yie. Another dorper followed him, then a third and a fourth.

There was no one present who failed to join the campaign for new light.

Led by Gui, Yie and Joa made trips deeper and deeper into the valleys to the west and east of Lake Digit, until they came to Lake Orteil. The terrain above the paths they took became rough and densely wooded. The pineries grew thicker. Wherever the three went, the belowers who heard them accepted the message they brought. Even the most conservative and traditional of the elderly agreed to help in the building of light screens that contained prismoids.

It was at the dorp called Besoin that the first trouble befell these evangelists of greater light. The small settlement, in the shadow of tall Enfer Mountain, was the scene of a confrontation with dangerous overtones.

A squad of four Red Hats stood at the door of the cottage where the dorpers had been listening to Yie and Joa present the program they were inviting the locals to join and support.

The two speakers, escorted by Gui, were preparing to leave when the door swung open and the four highlanders strode in. All eyes fastened on them.

The first Red Hat to enter spoke for the others.

"What is going on here? It appears to me that a number of strangers have arrived here in Besoin and are holding some sort of meeting with all the inhabitants. What is the business of these outsiders? What is their craft or trade? We have to find that out at once, because the Hegumen of Enfer claustrum is alarmed by this unusual activity. He demands to know the nature of what is going on. Is anything being bought or sold between the dorpers and these visitors? He demands to know the nature of any such exchange. Is there anything transpiring against the interest of the conventicle community on the summit of Enfer Mountain? Tell me what I have come here to find out. The truth about these activities must be revealed. There can be no secrecy on such an important matter."

Silence fell throughout the large room that took up most of the cottage. Uneasiness rose among all present. The mood grew tense.

At last. Gui took the initiative of answering the Red Hat.

"Let me introduce myself. I am the owner of the guest hotel on Lake Digit. My mission in Besoin is a very simple one. Let me explain it to your satisfaction, so that this inquiry of yours can be ended.

"I have guests staying with me from far away who have never been in or seen a northern dorp. These two with me tonight are interested in the folk traditions of the belower people. They asked me to take them to some interesting place where they could converse with and ask questions of northerners. I decided that there were few locations as picturesque and quaint as Besoin. So, the last several hours my customers have been talking with these dorpers about folk customs and traditions."

The leader of the Red Hats stared daggers at Gui, then turned his eyes on the other two. He looked long at Joa, then addressed Yie.

"What do you take us for? Do you think we are idiots? We have had our eyes on your gang for some time. Visits to a number of dorfs in the region have occurred. Meetings that last for hours. What is being said, what is being discussed?

"Do not try to tell me lies. You must give the absolute truth at this moment, or else there will be measures taken at once. Do you understand?"

Yie looked back at him without emotion.

"What can I tell you? Gui has given you the truth. There is nothing I can add to what has already been said."

The Red Hat's rising anger and indignation boiled over.

"Very well, then. I gave you a chance to tell an honest account. We know that you are agitators, but cannot determine the exact nature or the purpose of your activity. So, I must now take the three of you into police custody."

"Custody?" reacted Yie with genuine shock. "What do you mean by that?"

"The three of you will be escorted to the peak of Enfer, to our claustrum. The purpose is your questioning and interrogation under the Hegumen's direct control. Do not blame anyone but yourselves for this. It has become necessary because of the criminality of what you have been doing. The responsibility for all this is yours, not ours."

No one replied to the Red Hat's statements.

What could anyone have said?

The three visitors exited the cottage as prisoners. They had no idea what was going to happen to them in the immediate future.

Chapter III

The claustrum atop Enfer Mountain consisted of a walled inner structure with four separate wings. Like the rest of the high altitude, there was pure white snow covering the roofs and the grounds. Like hundred of similar Red Hat claustra on Tegumen, this one consisted of the privileged elite who ruled and exploited the belowers beneath them in the valleys. It was a cloistered, separated community of the favored beneficiaries of the planetary system.

The trio of prisoners shivered as they were marched into the fortress-like settlement. Their guards moved them toward a corridor at the center. The group entered the private quarters of the conventicle's Hegumen. Patiently standing at attention, the captured threesome waited while the leader of the Red Hats who had brought them there stepped behind a pine screen for a conference with someone unseen, probably the chief official on the mountain top.

The nerves of all three of them shook and rang as their fate was decided behind the partition. Joa and Yie looked at each other, not uttering a word. Their communication was inaudible, but comprehended by both of them. They both realized that their fate was being decided and determined.

All at once, the Red Hat who had arrested them returned, accompanied by a corpulent white-haired man in an orange tunic with the same color pants. The three prisoners knew instantly that this was the Hegumen himself, the one who managed and governed this claustrum on the mountain top.

The heavy man made an inspection of first Yie, then Joa and Gui.

"My name is Tiso," said the one in orange, "and I am commander of this conventicle and all who belong to it. In other words, I am Hegumen and am to be addressed as such.

"Now, it is absolutely necessary for me to know who each of you are and what you were up to in the dorp where our Brothers apprehended you. Is that clear? I must find out the truth about what you were up to. You must be completely candid with me."

Yie decided to take on the task of replying first.

"I can speak for the three of us, sir. We were in Besoin for legitimate, justifiable reasons. We are at present residing at the hotel on the shore of Lake Digit. The owner of the facility, Gui, is here with my partner and me. The purpose of our expedition is to meet with the dorpers of these valleys and ask them questions we are curious about. That is all. There is no illicit trade or exchange involved. We mean to delve into the traditions of this dorp, that is all. We are anxious to learn the patterns of their culture. The folkways of Besoin are the sole factor bringing us there."

The fat man took his time, sizing up the clever stranger he faced.

"Give me your names, please," he loudly ordered the three.

Yie, then Joa and Gui, did exactly that.

Tiso closely examined each of them as they gave their names, attempting to interpret their postures and expressions. Was it enough to make a judgment with? It could only serve as a start perhaps. He realized he had to delve deeper.

"Tell me, what portion of the culture in the dorps are you interested in? Can you describe the specific subjects that draw you?"

"Our particular curiosity centers on questions and problems of light," answered Yie. "What could be more crucial to the life of these people?"

The Hegumen knitted his broad brow. "I don't understand," he muttered. "Why should anyone be interested in such nonsense? The dorpers have no special knowledge of light. They see little of it, any way."

"In fact, that is what I most wish to find out: how the dorpers adjust to the paucity of light during their day and night. How do they make up for this lack of light? What compensations do they have to create for the darkness around them? How do they adjust themselves to the scarcity of light in their valleys?"

Tiso gazed with wonder at the captive before him.

"What is it to you what these people down below think about something as insubstantial as light? Why can such a thing be so important for you? I do not understand what you are trying to do. Your actions do not make sense to me at all."

Yie thought rapidly. He had to find an explanation that did not expose the secret project they had begun at Lake Digit.

It was going to be a difficult task for him. What was he going to say?

"Our aim is to explore the memories of the dorpers throughout the northern latitudes. What are their historical remembrances? We believe that there are valuable treasures there that can be applied to the future. That is all we went to Besoin for. Nothing beyond that," lied Yie as convincingly as he could.

This is the only way out of here for us, the visionary told himself. Only a fiction can shield us from the highlander's wrath and vengeance.

The truth cannot set us free, only credible falsehood will do the trick. We have no alternative to use of innocent, necessary subterfuge.

Tiso then gave his solemn decision as if he were a judge.

"For now, we shall be your hosts and provide comfortable rooms for each of you. Please, do not try to leave. It is a hard path down into the valley where you were found and arrested."

With that, the round man in orange walked away and disappeared behind the pine partition.

The prisoners were taken off to their new quarters at once.

Food was bought to each chamber for the three to eat. It was tasty and adequate, furnished to the claustrum by its subordinate dorps and hamlets.

It was after their keepers had left that Yie went into the room assigned to Joa. The two were soon joined by Gui.

"What shall we do now?" asked a worried Joa. "Can we hide all our plans for long? What if they torture us to make us talk?"

Gui tried to give her encouragement. "If we stick to what Yie has said, Tiso will have to relent in time. It is a matter of patiently resisting him, but we can win by being consistent in all our answers and statements. Isn't that so, Yie?"

The latter nodded. "Exactly. Persistence will make us victorious. We have no alternative way of getting away from here."

Joa looked directly at Yie. "I can see the wisdom of such a course. But won't it take a considerable time before our captor is convinced and compelled to release us?"

Yie reached out and took her hand in his.

"Time is on our side, Joa, if we say the same thing to him again and again. We went to Besoin to collect ancient folklore. We admit nothing beyond that."

"Will the Hegumen accept such an explanation, though?"

The two exchanged deep, fixed looks.

"We can say nothing else, my love," whispered the belower to the highlander.

The snow that fell that night began as small pellets of grampel. It continued and came without pause. After a time, this became a fluffy neige of large, cottony flakes that formed a thick mantle over the top of Enfen Mountain. The peak was transformed by this change. It became a realm of conquering whiteness.

Yie woke hours before dawn and looked out to see that the building he was in was entrapped in deep, enveloping white.

We are not the only ones imprisoned here, he thought with irony.

Tiso is holding us, but the snow is marooning him and his people as well.

In a while, the scraping noise of shovels became audible.

What next? wondered Yie. The Hegumen has something in store for us. Is our strength up to the task of withstanding whatever happens? Will it prove adequate? He prepared himself to learn what Tiso was going to do with them.

Frelo and Cacique were seriously concerned. Why hadn't the three come back? What had happened to block their return to Lake Digit?

The two town-dwellers considered what to do as they watched the heliac rise over the placid waters. They stood facing each other on the veranda of the hotel. Both were in a quandary.

"Maybe we should go out and trace their route," suggested Carique, a worried expression on his face.

"What if we try that and get lost out there between the mountains?" said the theater director. "How can that help them get back?"

Cacique bit his lip. "So, what do we do, at least for today?"

Frelo shrugged his shoulders. "What is there for us but to wait?"

Cacique made a wry smile. "We can think about what action we may have to take if they do not return soon."

At long last a lead had come his way. Nomb Aacn sat back in the chair that once had held the qadic. He now acted as supreme magistrate and the Red Hats had full control and authority to search, investigate, and arrest.

Days of probing and hunting had led to one simple conclusion: the fugitives were no longer anywhere about, not in that region of the planet at all.

Where had they escaped to?

No one had any idea till a rumor arrived over the Red Hat grapevine.

A traveling Brother from a far northern claustrum had heard from someone else who had picked up word from a another traveler...

Nomb looked down and read the terse report.

"A small group of southern persons are staying at one of the Digit Lakes, acting suspiciously and drawing attention to themselves."

That was all the information it contained. Should he send someone there to look into this group?

No, decided the Hegumen from Zeviv Mountain.

He would journey north himself and look into what the report suspected to be present there.

Chapter IV

The Brothers went about their tasks of restoring life to the claustrum after the blizzard of snowfall ended. Breakfast was brought to the three prisoners, and Yie was told that he was to meet with a person who wished to see him.

Who could that be? wondered the captive as he finished eating his bowl of burghul. Was a new series of interrogations going to begin with an unnamed questioner? He would have to wait to see who the instrument of the Hegumen turned out to be.

Joa and Gui were told that something new was about to happen to Yie. Shortly after, the Red Hats came to take him to the far end of the settlement. Guards escorted him along a covered outer corridor, then ordered Yie to enter a room through a quercine door.

Once inside, the prisoner saw a small figure, a dwarflike person with tiny legs and arms, sitting at a low, benchlike table.

"Sit down," commanded the tiny man in a high, fluttering voice.

When Yie had done so, he stared into the milky eyes of the strange creature. Why had the Hegumen summoned him to meet such a disfigured form as this?

The man behind the table began to address him.

"My name is Eter. I am Chief Mechanician of this settlement. That makes me the one in charge of energy works and devices. All magnetics fall under my purview. I am the one who enables the conventicle to use light rays from the sky for practical purposes. That is my main responsibility."

The pair stared searchingly at each other for a time. At last, Yie felt he had to ask the question weighing on him.

"Can you enlighten me as to why I was brought to meet with you?"

"I saw the Hegumen early this morn. He informed me on how you were found with the belowers of the dorp Besoin and brought up here. The chief of our claustrum was dissatisfied with the answers given by you and your two companions. The session with the villagers was, according to you, involved with folklore legends of some sort. That is what you claim is the truth.

"Late last evening, after the three of you returned to your rooms, one of our Brothers remembered something that had, in the crush of action, been momentarily forgotten and not recalled. Twice, the man said, he had heard you mention light. Why was that so? I was told to ask of you. Was it folk traditions concerned with light that you were trying to elicit from these belowers? What did you learn from the people in Besoin? Were you attempting to provoke dissention somehow?

"Since I am a specialist on cosmic radiation, the task was assigned me. I have to find out what your expedition in the valley has to do with light. What sort of light were you discussing when our Brothers placed you under arrest? Why such great interest in that particular subject?"

Yie had a sense of great unease. What was he to say to this? How was he to conceal the nature of his ultimate project from these Red Hats?

His words carefully weighed and measured, Yie answered as best he could. He hoped to put off the little technician with clever diversions.

"I have always been interested in the subject of light, and our legends and history tell me that the inhabitants of all our valleys share in that. So, I was trying to learn how various dorps in different valleys cope with their lack of heliac light. That is, I tried to find out what are the explanations of the situation of inadequate illumination, of the severe shortness of the day. There are numerous, varying legends in different places. That was what we were after. That was the ultimate goal of our journey."

"I see," said Eter in a surprisingly low, guttural tone. "But what did you learn from the inhabitants of Besoin? And why did it take so long to glean that from the dorpers?"

Yie attempted a disarming smile.

"It is not easy to get belowers to reveal matters like that. We had to let them discourse on and on at extraordinary length. The talkers that we found here were loquacious, digressing far afield. Much time was wasted on trivial subjects before we brought them to the main topic."

"Which was light," smiled the little man.

"Correct. It took hours of effort before the dam broke. Then, a flood of information was transmitted to us."

"Tell me the nature of what they revealed, please," insisted Eter, his voice surprisingly firm and strong.

Yie decided that he had to spin a fable for his interrogator.

"At one time far back in the forgotten past, all the migrants to this world of Tegumen lived where light was shared by all. Where it penetrated both deep valleys and the highest mountain tops. Shadow was only temporary. Hours of illumination equaled those of darkness. There were no hours of murky twilight, without true day. Both those high and those low possessed light in equal measure. All people enjoyed its benefits on the same level.

"But then came catastrophic inner explosions and eruptions of their planet, till it no longer was habitable. The time came when all recognized they had to escape. So, using skycraft of all sorts, the population went out to seek a new planetary home far away, among strange stars. They could not remain where they were any longer.

"Tegumen was the chosen destination. But it was the piloting crews who made this specific decision. The reason for that has been lost in the mists of history. The belowers suspect that what happened was that the navigators and their families took the mountain peaks for themselves, settling the bulk of the passengers as tillers and herders in the lower elevations of this planet of uplands and valleys.

"Thus, some came to have a number of times the light of others. The mechanisms of optical exploitation remained on top with the descendants of the sky crews, while the passenger population was assigned to the shadows in the valleys.

"That was what we had learned from the dorpers when the Red Hats placed the three of us under arrest and brought us up here."

"Was that all that was related to you in Besoin?" inquired Eter. "Was there nothing said about legends concerning future times? Did they convey to you what they believed about what is going to be in time to come?"

Yie thought fast, hunting for a way to take the little man off the scent of what he was concealing. "We never reached that time, not at all. Everything the dorpers said concerned the far distant past, not the present or near times."

"But different people perceive that same past differently," mused the mechanicist. "It is one history for some, another for others, depending upon where they are located. Do you understand what I am saying to you?"

"I'm not at all sure. Can you be more specific about what you mean?" countered the prisoner.

Eter gave a laugh, then went on to provide some kind of an answer.

"Our perspective of how light is distributed cannot be the same as the one you claim to have found down in Besoin. When the migrants arrived this far, they had no choice but to land on Tegumen. You see, their fuel was exhausted and there was no way to renew it. So, this had to be the planet for landing and settlement.

"The terrain was unlike that of our previous home, of course. A new adaptation was necessary, for both crew and passengers. They had to organize their life into a system unfamiliar to everyone who descended here. The energy rays that fell on the high mountain zone had to be tamed and utilized. This became the specialty of our technicals who had control of the vehicular engines of our space vessels. Their knowledge was then transferred to Tegumen and its unique conditions. They set up our present system that uses galactic rays to produce iotic power. The passengers who became the new world's belowers were sent down into the valleys, since they could not take command of any type of energy by themselves. A more primitive, simpler life remained available for them. With time, their hamlets and villages were able to sustain cities based on crafts and commerce. But the photonic science remained the special preserve of those who from the first inhabited the highest places, the peaks where light shined the most."

"Must the Red Hats, then, consider all others to be inferiors?" murmured Yie.

Eter made a sour face of distaste. "No, that is not the necessary result of these conditions. The belowers are only somewhat different from us. That is so because of the unique environment we dwell in. That is the reason for the enormous divide between us."

Yie found himself saying what might lead to trouble for him. He grew increasingly anxious as he expressed his thoughts.

"But couldn't the rays of the heliac be somehow harnessed by those at lower levels? Perhaps not in the past or the present, but someday yet to come? Isn't that a possibility in their legends and folklore?"

"I do not know if it is or isn't. Have you come upon anything of that nature in your travels through the valleys?"

The face of Yie reddened. What was he to say? Eter had put him in a position difficult to squirm out of without making too much visible and evident. The prisoner groped for an answer.

"One never knows with these dorpers, sir. When they speak of the far distant past, their thoughts may be focused on the present or the future. Their minds are dense forests, full of snarls and tangles of all sorts."

The mechanicist stared at Yie with opaque milky eyes.

"I guess what you say about these people is true. But they are experts at concealment and subterfuge. They may have been pulling your leg, as well as those of your companions. Is there anything else of importance they may have said to you about the subject of light?"

"Not that I can immediately think of," prevaricated the prisoner. "If I remember anything more, it will certainly be brought forward by me."

"You can go back to your quarters now," commanded Eter, looking away to the side as if unwilling to look any longer at a person he was certain was not telling him the truth.

Chapter V

The crepuscular shadows of evening were creeping over Lake Digit almost inperceptively. Cacique and Flero sat together on the veranda of the hotel, discussing the dilemma they shared. Both of them were experiencing a sense of vague alarm.

"What are we going to do?" asked the designer, sitting beside the director. "Yie, Joa, and Gui are out there in a valley, yet we have no communication from them at all. My fear is that something terrible has befallen them. I can only guess at what it might be."

Flero turned his eyes on his friend and partner.

"If we remain uncertain, there is nothing definite for us to do. If we decide on any one alternative, it may turn out the worst one of all, though."

"Then, we have to remain inactive?"

"At times, that is the only rational way to deal with a situation without clear contours. How else can we meet our dilemma, Cacique?"

The latter did not reply, his eyes catching a distant shadow.

Flero, noticing this stare, also looked in that direction.

Both men clearly distinguished a short line of equines, in which rode a number of riders wearing red-colored headgear. The first of those watching to say anything was Cacique.

"They will soon be here at the hotel. What can we do?"

Flero answered at once with a specific plan he thought up at the moment, as if in an instant.

"No one knows you are here. I plan to stay in the hotel and attempt to confuse and delay the Red Hats. That should give you time to run away with a head start. Do you understand? It is your duty to find the others and warn them about the appearance of our mortal enemies. The responsibility for this will be yours. Their future safety and well-being will be in your hands."

Cacique hesitated only a second.

"It is perhaps a wild hope, that of locating our friends, but I will attempt to accomplish it. Good-bye for now, Flero. I think it wisest to take the path away from the lake, heading westward into the valleys. Good-bye, my friend. Until we see each other again."

"We shall come together again," Flero assured him. "I am certain that we shall."

Yie met with Joa and Gui in the room occupied by the latter.

All three kept their voices low, fearing someone would overhear.

"I can see some hope of our being released," whispered Yie, "if it is possible to move the conscience of the tiny man called Eter. And I believe that he could convince Hegumen Tiso that there is no danger to him and his authority from any of us. That appears possible to me."

The next to give an opinion was Joa.

"Yes, I know how it is with high officials like my father. They do not give any ear to outsiders, only trusted members of their own claustrum."

"It will be a risky operation for you," noted Gui. "What if the mechanician reacts negatively to proposals to liberate us?"

Yie thought a moment. "I must be very careful not to provoke the little man. A lot of thought has to be taken about how to approach and handle him. I have told the Brothers watching over us that I wish to talk with him sometime today."

"Let's allow Yie to think out what strategy to follow, Gui," said Joa, her brow furrowed with worry. A great gamble lay ahead for them, they all realized.

Yie decided that their only chance for successful release lay with the mechanician named Eter. He asked to see him again, and was escorted to the small man's quarters by the Red Hats guarding him and his two companions.

Once they were seated, Yie started off with a brazen, provocative question. "Tell me, do you harbor hatred for the belowers of the valleys?"

The answer came slowly and grudgingly.

"Of course, I do not. At least that is what my conscious mind says to me. Yet I realize how much animus there is among many of my Brothers. I cannot measure how much of it may have seeped into me without my being aware of it. That can happen unconsciously without knowing it. That is a possibility. I don't know if I can accept it as the truth.

"So I claim that I nurse no hatred for them, but question whether I am perfectly certain of it. Why did you ask me that?"

Yie posed a further question, not giving the other an answer.

"Would you oppose me and my friends should we attempt to bring the benefits of heliac light to the people of the lowlands? What would your reaction to it be?"

Eter became visibly agitated. His hands and fingers shook for several seconds. A shadow seemed to fall over his grayish face.

"Such a thought has never occurred to me. Excuse me if I hesitate to give an immediate answer. My feeling is this: I know that it would be wrong for me or anyone else to harm the belowers by forcing them to continue to live in so much darkness as they now do. But would I be willing to take any positive action on their behalf? That is hard to say. All that I am certain of at the moment is that I would not stand in the way of their progress and well-being. That could not be justified in any way.

"But why are you asking such a speculative question? What you propose is not possible, is it?"

He looked at Yie with a searching expression, not sure what the prisoner might say in reply.

"I do not know as much about high optics as you do," said Yie slowly, cautiously, "but others have demonstrated for me how the valleys of our planet may one day be provided a longer period of illumination at all levels, in all the regions. That could enable us to exploit the rays of our heliac, the way that the Red Hats of the mountain claustra use galactic rays from space for the iotic power that they generate."

Eter grew excited, forgetting that he was supposed to be questioning the outsider about a completely different matter.

"The idea you describe is not entirely new to me," responded the highlander. "In my own mental wanderings, I have many times imagined Tegumen different in relation to heliac light. If only we knew how to bend the corpuscula descending from out of the sky. If only we were able to transmit it where we wished.

"But why waste our thoughts on what is impossible to achieve?"

The two were silent for a few moments, until Yie took up the challenge the other had presented him by his last statement.

"What if the angling of light is possible, using the right instruments?"

Ester made a grimace that reflected his doubts. "Pardon me, but your words sound absurdly preposterous to me," he declared.

"What if the corpuscles of light were reflected in a new direction? What if their angle could be changed to a different one?"

"No mirror that large can be constructed," asserted the expert mechanician. "It would have been done by now, were it possible."

"There is a way to bend heliac light without the use of any mirror," said Yie in a level, controlled tone. "I know how it can be done."

All at once, the diminutive Eter rose out of his low chair and stepped toward the man who appeared to be teasing him.

"I cannot compel or force you to tell me," pleaded the runt-like scientist. "All I can do is to beg you to reveal what you think can be done."

He looked at Yie with complete concentration, as if having forgotten what his role was supposed to be.

Realizing that he was now in control of the situation, Yie began to toy with the small one.

"I ask myself this: can I trust any Red Hat with that knowledge? Might it not turn out to be a big mistake to reveal what I know? There are considerations that make me hesitate to do so."

He gazed at the Red Hat with intense concentration.

"I will not mishandle that knowledge if you share it with me," solemnly promised Eter. "My word can be trusted and depended on. I am not a person who breaks confidences given by others."

Looking with confidence at the little man, Yie suddenly beamed a smile.

"A prismoid with a certain deviation can send a load of corpuscula in a specified direction, bending vertical light in a horizontal direction. The most desirable result is totally polarized light which can spread and diffuse through any valley with any shape to it.

"If we create a prismoid with planes of light that come out in polarized form, we could direct the heliac rays at any oblique angle desired. A great number of these prismoids could send corpuscula at different angles, suffusing open space with polarized light. There would not remain a single situs not illuminated. They would be under total immersion of light.

"There, I have told you what I know to be possible."

Eter gazed down at the floor, not sure what to say or do.

"We must talk again soon," muttered the mechanician. "You have provided me much to think about. I thank you for your explanation. You will be informed once I have formed a definite decision."

Realizing he was being dismissed, Yie swiftly left the room. His mind was unable to gauge what effect his words might or might not have had on his listener, the mechanician.

Chapter VI

Cacique sped along with no heed to anything beyond getting to his lost comrades, somewhere in the vicinity of Lake Orteil. With the Red Hats of Nomb Aacn on his trail, he could afford no mistake in the path he took. A great quantity of luck was needed to take him to the location where he would find the three he meant to give a warning to.

As if by a directing intuition of some kind, the fleeing designer entered the valley to the east of Enfer Mountain. From time to time, the sound of thundering equine hooves could be heard in the distance. He continued on, seeking both information and protection in each dorp he passed through.

His situation became increasingly desperate and threatened.

Some interior sense informed Cacique he was near his goal. It was in the dorp of Soison, under the shadow of high Enfer Mountain, that he received confirmation of this feeling within him.

"They were here only days ago, and the leader spoke to us of the light from the lake that we might share in. But then the Red Hats came and took all three of them away up to the peak. That was the last we saw of them."

The dorper pointed to the top of the adjacent mountain.

"Thank you for what you have told me," said Cacique, his eyes staring up at the pure white snow of Enfer beyond the circular window.

He knew that instant where he had to go. But what could possibly be done by him to rescue the trio held up there at the mountain peak?

I will decide that when I reach the height, the fugitive said to himself.

Joa and Gui listened with astonishment to what Yie related to them. The three met in the back corridor behind their rooms.

"And he did not attack or disregard what you said to him?" inquired Joa, breathing rapidly with her emotions aroused.

"His reaction was very surprising," said Yie with all his mental force. "I did not expect such sudden, immediate interest. Everything was positive, nothing negative, in the attitude the man took. He showed enormous curiosity. His mind was fascinated by the picture I drew of the possibilities for the future. It was a big surprise to me, how he was reacting to the picture I described for him."

"But what will he do for us?" interceded Gui. "Will our situation as captives remain unchanged?"

Yie's face became a stony wall of flint.

"My suspicion is that he will go to the Hegumen with the material I gave him to think about. If he does that immediately, we could see some important changes. What way these go, depends on factors beyond us. The thoughts of the governor of the conventicle are unpredictable. No one knows where they will lead and where they will end up."

"How true!" exclaimed Joa, a wry expression on her face.

"Now," grimly said Yie, "we must wait to learn how this turns out."

Eter entered the private chamber of the Hegumen Tiso to make his report on the questioning of Yie. As soon as the two sat down, the mechanician began to describe the startling revelation he had heard.

"I was told of a technical development that this trio is involved with. It is something which, if successful, can turn life upside down for all the people on our planet. Do not laugh when you hear what it is. They are absolutely serious about their project. Their goal is to bring the light we enjoy on top of the mountains to the belowers in the valleys."

"What?" said Tiso, surprised and energized. "How do these people propose to accomplish that impossible task?"

"By bending the corpuscula of light falling from the heliac. They plan to build large reflective walls that deflect the particles into horizontal levels across the valleys.

"Yie claims that the process is proven to work. A type of prism called a prismoid is the basis for the invention. He told me that it has already been done on a small, test scale. The method applied was successful, the belower claimed."

"I do not find his claims credible," grumbled the Hegumen. "Not at all. You should let Yie know that I believe he is trying to pull my leg for some devious purpose. I suspect the man is a fraudulent imposter.

"I order you to take no stock in his fantasies. They have no value whatsoever. He must realize that he is not dealing with fools here on Enfin Mountain. He cannot hope to carry out any fraud or swindle on us."

Eter excused himself and departed, his mind caught in a dilemma.

His superior had given him a clear, direct command, and he intended to obey it.

But through his thinking resonated the voice of Yie, telling him of the glorious future of Tegumen that was to result from polarized, bent light produced by prismoids.

What was he to say to the stranger who had presented the enticing dream to him? How could he deny what was glowing so brightly in his imagination?

Eter decided not to reveal the negative judgment of Tiso to the prisoner who had given him the vision of a planet transformed through optical science. No, he planned to think this out for himself, not follow his leader blindly. It would take a lot of time and thought to reach any solid, valid conclusion.

Cacique trudged onward and upward with growing exhaustion, increasing his effort despite the pain expanding through his body.

He had learned that his friends had been taken prisoners by the Red Hats. What could one person do to rescue them? There was no ready answer to that.

The path he was on left the zone of conifers and entered an area of bare rock, then came to the white snow that covered the peak. As the drifts became deeper, Cacique had trouble striding forward. The coldness of the air and snow penetrated his light coat. He felt a painful chill.

What will I do when I reach my destination? he asked himself.

Never looking back or downwards, his eyes did not catch sight of the posse following him on equines.

The pursuers drew nearer as the claustrum became visible to the climber.

Nomb Aacn could see the moving object traversing the snow. His mind was perplexed. Why was this fugitive heading for a place where he must know he would be taken prisoner and given over to those he was running away from?

There is no use trying to understand the belowers, he once more concluded. They are dense and inexplicable. Do not be concerned with their cloudy, inexplicable thoughts.

Eter did not wait for Yie to be brought to him, but himself went to the section of the claustrum where prisoners were kept.

A Red Hat guard informed him in which room Yie stayed. Eter went up to it and rapped on the hornbeam door with all his might.

Opening it, Yie gave a start of surprise upon seeing who it was.

"Come in," he succeeded in gasping.

The little mechanician entered. Yie invited him to sit down, but Eter said he would not be there long and preferred to stand rather than take a seat.

"I have spoken to the Hegumen about what you revealed to me," said Eter. "No final decision can be reached at this time. We will need to mount a demonstration of how these prismoids work. Is that possible?"

The eyes of Yie expanded and dilated. "There is nothing that we brought with us. I would have to return to Lake Digit to obtain what is needed to accomplish that."

Eter thought a moment. "I shall present the matter to our Hegumen. If he agrees, you can leave and the other two remain here. As soon as possible, I aim to tell him of a demonstration before his own eyes. That will interest him greatly. I know that for certain."

With that, the little mechanician turned around and left the room.

The front gate of the summit settlement loomed ahead as Cacique panted and raced toward it. He dared not look behind. The noise of hooves sounded in his ears. A single neigh revealed that equines were pursuing behind him.

Toward the quercine portal rushed the stage designer.

What would he do when he reached it? Could he open it by himself?

It would be horrible if the gate was locked from the inside.

Would anyone show him mercy and admit him into the conventicle?

The mind of Cacique whirled dizzily, till consciousness and balance reached a tipping point.

A sound unlike anything he had ever experienced struck and felled him. A shot from a carabine rifle struck the back of his neck and decided his future.

One of the pursuing Red Hats had fired from an equine, putting an end to further movement of any kind by the individual who had first devised the prismoid invention.

Chapter VII

Three guards from within the claustrum were the first to reach the fallen body and examine it for signs of life. The pursuing posse only arrived after Hegumen Tiso walked out of the gate to investigate the shooting noise that had broken the silence of the summit. What could it have been? Who was causing the loud, awful sound?

Nomb Aacn identified himself to the head of the community.

"We have been chasing a criminal fugitive who attempted to enter your fortress," he explained. "That was a horrendous mistake on the part of one of my subordinates. He shall be punished for this act of his, because it is now impossible to question the belower he brought down."

The mind of Tiso was working faster than that of the other abbotial.

"It is best that this seriously wounded person be carried at once into the claustrum for treatment of his injury. I have people skilled in the surgical arts who will take care of him." He looked past Nomb at the large contingent of mounted Red Hats. "We do not have space or supplies for so many guests. There can only be a single person admitted and taken care of. That will be you, sir. The others must return to whatever shelter can be found for them in the valley, not here on Mt. Enfin. First of all, we must take care of the fallen one. Please order some equine-riders to return below while it is still twilight. Is that clear?"

Tiso turned about to watch his men pick up and carry off the unconscious body of Cacique. He followed this small group as Nomb dismissed his group of Red Hats.

I shall hunt for my daughter within these walls, the Hegumen of Zeviv said to himself as he followed the rescuers through the gate into the claustrum.

As soon as he heard the carabine's report, Yie rushed out into the corridor. Joa and Gui soon joined him there.

"What was that?" asked the young woman.

"Both of you must stay here while I try to investigate," her lover told her. "I will ask the Brothers guarding us first. They should know what it was."

The Red Hats, excited and confused, were not able to tell him anything.

Yie, thinking fast, came up with a request that might be acceptable to the two.

"I must see Eter, the mechanician, at once. There is no time to lose. He can find out what the noise was better than any of us."

Surprisingly, the Brothers guarding the prisoners were so disoriented that they accepted this proposed method of learning what the situation was.

Within less than a minute, Yie had been escorted to the door of the chamber occupied by the tiny Eter.

A knock on the door by one of the Red Hats brought no reply.

"He is not here. Perhaps the man has gone to see what the trouble is," concluded one of the Brothers.

"But he will return," opined Yie. "I must stay here till Eter is back. You can leave me here, I cannot run off anywhere with all the snowfall around the summit. It is impossible for anyone to flee."

The Red Hats exchanged looks, then walked away, leaving Yie as the only figure outside the rooms of the technical.

Eter, with some knowledge of the human body, aided the medico in treating the wounded man. Guards had carried him into the personal quarters of Hegumen Tiso, who had secretly issued orders that Nomb Aacn was to be kept from entering these chambers. A chamber had been assigned to him, together with three Brothers to see after his immediate needs. He was to be watched and followed at all times, Tiso had commanded. He was not to be permitted to walk about on his own or investigate conditions concerning the other visitors within the claustrum.

It was only after the successful removal of the ball lodged in the neck of the victim that Eter had the opportunity to return to his own rooms.

"The patient needs a lot of sleep and rest," said the medico after placing a strong soporific pill in the mouth of the injured Cacique.

Eter left, going back to his quarters with slow, tired steps. He picked up his pace when he spotted Yie standing at his door.

"What has happened?" asked the one waiting there, the fugitive.

"Let's go in and talk," said the short mechanician. "There is a very complicated story to relate. It will take some time."

Once both of them were seated and the explanation began.

Yie gaped for breath as he heard the name of the Hegumen from Zeviv. He interrupted the narrator with a question.

"The Red Hat official is no longer surrounded by his mounted guards?"

"No. He is under watch in one of the office rooms of our own Hegumen. Special guest quarters are being prepared for him. He is not in a position to wander or look around on his own."

"Could you please describe the man who was shot? I may be able to identify who he is."

"He is large and very heavy. His hair is red and curly, and his eyes are a leaden gray."

In an instant, Yie identified Cacique, the stage lighting designer.

"You must take me at once to your Hegumen. I can tell him who this fallen person is. And there is much that I know about the misdeeds connected with the high official who is here now. I must warn this community of the character of their visitor. He has a dangerous aura about him. All of you must know why he is carrying out his horrible hunt through the mountains in search of me and my companions."

Eter studied the face of his new friend for a moment.

"Come along with me. This matter cannot wait."

The two of them quickly hurried out, the small one leading the way with unbelievably speedy steps.

Hegumen Tiso sat stupefied, listening to the tale told him by Yie. Only after the latter finished did the head of the claustrum turn to his mechanician with a pointed question.

"Is this fellow making up a bizzare story to fool us into something, or is he credible in all he says? Has the governor of the Zeviv conventicle acted so monstrously toward this pair, their friends, and untold belowers? Has he become a merciless pursuer and torturer?"

Eter looked his superior straight in the eye.

"I fall on the side of belief. And there is a way to check up on him. Have the daughter brought here to you and question her yourself. Even the smallest difference in what the two say can provide ground for doubt and suspicion on your part. Then conduct your own examination of her account of what has happened. See whether these stories coincide."

Tiso, pondering hard for a while, made an irreversible decision.

"I will have the young woman brought here. You can take Yie to your quarters and keep him there until I have use for him. For now, that is all."

Eter and Yie rose and departed as ordered.

Joa related exactly the same series of events that Tiso had already heard. Every fact and detail matched. No more questions were needed. The truth was plainly evident for him to see and understand for himself.

The next step was clear to the Hegumen of Enfin. He had summoned Eter and gave him specific, drastic orders to carry out.

"First of all, take the most recent guest, the official, to come here and escort him down to the locked barracoon. He is to be kept prisoner there until I can arrange a trial by a united court of all the claustra of our northern zone. The charges against him will be serious ones, with grave penalties resulting from his conviction.

"Then, bring the man named Yie back to me. I have important plans to work out with him."

These commands were carried out with rapid, unprecedented precision.

Chapter VIII

The quick, efficient trial of Nomb Aacn was over within a single day.

Testimony against the accused came from both Hie and his daughter Joa. Evidence of his criminal use of power in Rocumbol was abundant, as well as his assaults on the belowers of Caldaria.

His judges decided on life imprisonment as fitting punishment for the harm he had caused to others, including his only child, Joa.

Hegumen Tiso agreed to keep him confined in an escape-proof oubliette with only a small door on its roof. Escape from the claustrum nearest to Digit Lake was considered all but impossible. No one could break in or out of the high mountain fortress. The father of Joa became a forgotten personality, buried in faint memories of the harm and pain he had caused for so many.

A new Hegumen was selected to rule and reform the Zeviv claustrum. Major reorganization and devolution of power and authority occurred at once. The institution was totally restructured. In future days, no single individual would amass the power and authority that Nomb Aacn had abused for personal purposes.

Yie and Joa decided that they would make a permanent residence for themselves at Lake Digit, near the hotel of their friend Gui and facing the heliac-illuminated waters. It was the location both of them preferred to live at. It reminded both of them of the great plasmoid invention and the profound social and economic changes that would result from this revolutionary new technology once it was tested, proven, and placed into practical application over the entire planet.

"I have to be available for work on our experimental screens of prismoids. That is going to become the central activity of my life," Yie told Joa and the recovering Cacique once their lives had fallen into an ordered daily routine.

The three sat on the veranda of the Digit Lake Hotel, gazing at the setting of the heliac into the mountains soaring up to the west.

"How many years will it take to reach tangible results?" asked Joa. "When shall the belowers of our valleys see changes in their everyday lives as the silver platinum plates now in production are distributed over Tegumen so that the heliac light caught by the prismoids becomes available to all of our valleys?"

The surface of the lake glistened with brilliant blood red light as Cacique replied.

"No one can calculate how many years or generations it will take. Perhaps an entire epoch of time is needed. But now that we have the Enfin claustrum on our side, the road ahead will be clear and open for us. One by one, all the other highland communities are giving in to the inevitable. There is a new, unprecedented recognition and respect for the belowers who have created an entirely new form of iotic energy from the rays of our heliac. There will no longer exist the age-old system of technical monopoly exercised by the Red Hats in their mountain-top claustra. That is over for good."

Joa smiled. "In time, our whole planet will enjoy the light that only the mountain peaks and a few northern lakes enjoyed until our generation."

"That is our covenant with the future," smiled Yie. "One day, all the valleys will be lighted up.

"I thought that I had found the genuine solution to the needs of the valleys in the old manuscript that described the use of silver platinum plates in the old planetary home. That did not prove to be the simple answer for Tegumen, but at least it put me on the road to the goal. The old system that had been in use on the home planet could not be created anew here on our world. So, it was the concept proposed by Cacique, the prismoidals, that gave us the method that led to this technical victory. We owe the success to you, Cacique. You are the one who brought the crucial addition to what were the silver platinum plates that worked once back on another planet that our ancestors had to leave."

The lighting technician smiled with joy. "It all happened by lucky chance, I believe. The origin of the prismoids occurred in stagecraft, but then they moved into the area of light-based energy. It was a very fortunate coincidence for all of us on our planet that it occurred."

Each of them concentrated on the dream of the shining future that they shared. In time to come, light and its energy would be a resource shared in common all over the mountains and valleys of Tegumen. The valleys would escape their long, painful darkness.

The End

Lightning Source UK Ltd.
Milton Keynes UK
UKHW011013210820
368606UK00001B/81